REAL MONSTERS

~ LIAM BROWN ~

Legend Press Ltd, The Old Fire Station,
140 Tabernacle Street, London, EC2A 4SD
info@legend-paperbooks.co.uk | www.legendpress.co.uk

 British Library Cataloguing in Publication Data available.

Print ISBN 978-1-9103945-6-4
Ebook ISBN 978-1-9103945-7-1
Set in Times. Printed in the United Kingdom by Clays Ltd.
Cover design by Simon Levy www.simonlevyassociates.co.uk

After leaving school, **Liam Brown** spent five years working a series of increasingly mundane jobs, including burger flipper, helium balloon pedlar and a two-month stint manning the shooting alley at a travelling fairground. After eighteen months travelling and working in the Philippines, he returned to the UK and began writing stories.

Liam is the lead singer and guitarist in the band Freelance Mourners. He lives in Birmingham with his wife and two children.

Real Monsters is his debut novel.

Follow Liam
@LiamBrownWriter

For Tony and George. Sleep tight.

ONE

This ain't no fuckin beach. Nah. Sure there's sand. Sand like you wouldn't believe – and different types too. It's like they say about the eskimos havin all them different words for snow. Only with sand. I've become quite the expert. You got the fine powdery sort. That's the shit that gets lifted by the wind and whips in your eyes and mouth so that you end up grinding the grit between your back teeth. Like you're chewin on a bone or somethin. Then there's the thick, sticky stuff. The shit that'll suck off your boot and sock as you're tryna climb a dune. Like glue it is. Take your whole leg if you're not lucky – I've seen it. I swear that shit's magnetically charged. Clumps together and covers your skin like a layer of bad paint. A white man'll come out black after a bad enough storm. Or vice-a-versa I guess, ha.

That's another thing no one tells ya. The colours. There's more variation than you'd think. First off you got your whites. Like salt or sugar it is, the light bouncing back so bright it burns your eyes – whites so white it ain't no colour at all, more like a billion bits of crushed up crystal. Like you're yompin over glass or somethin. Course there's your off-whites too. Them's more common. Your creams, greys, all the way down to your blacks. The dirty-lookin business like soiled, week-old snow. Hate it, I do. Sods law says that's the shit you end up hackin up from the back of your throat after you get caught out in a bad'un. I swear the first few times you think you're coughin up a tumour ha. Then you got your browns – wheat, rye, millet, oat – a whole fuckin spectrum of cereals, like you're walkin through breakfast.

And then there're your reds. Them's my favourite, the reds. Rarest too. Days are you walk for hours and see nothin but shitty greys and tarry blacks. Then all of a sudden you come over a hill and there it is – an endless stretch of the stuff, shimmerin in the sun like a whole fuckin ocean of blood. It takes your breath away, it really does.

Anyways, the reason I was writin was I got your picture and I wanted to say thanks. I got it taped to the inside of my tent, so it's the first thing I see when I open my eyes each mornin and the last thing I see before I go to sleep each night. That's how much I like it. You're writin your name now I see? Well good on ya. That's all a man needs to sign his life away ha. But really it's good. I was twice your age when I learnt to write my name, so you keep it up. Like I said before, you're man of the house now. It's important you keep up the learnin. Don't have your head in the books too much, mind. Ain't no matter how smart you are when some little whatsit pulls a knife on you and tries to slit your gullet open. Think you're gonna spell your way out of it?

What I'm trying to say is that it's all about balance. You need to be rounded. Sure you can read your books, but kick a ball now and then. And do a few push-ups while you're at it. No one wants to be the skinny kid. They're always the first to get their teeth smashed in.

There was one other thing about your picture. And I'm not havin a go. Like I said, I've got it taped up and everythin. I even shown a couple of the lads. But there's somethin been buggin me about it. I couldn't put my finger on it at first, and then it hit me. It's that big lick of blue you got down the one side. I mean, at first I thought it was the wind or somethin, that maybe you were tryna be a little abstract. But then I looked a little closer and there's no mistakin it. You can even see the little splashes of white, like the crests of waves rollin and breakin on the shore. It's the sea. And then I started lookin even harder and I saw you'd done the sand in yellow.

Not white or brown, but yellow. Golden even, with a row of little bumps that look a whole lot like sandcastles from where I'm sittin. Christ, you've even got a fuckin palm tree on there.

Now I don't know what your mother's told ya, but there ain't no palm trees out here, son. There ain't no sea and there certainly ain't no sandcastles. All that's here is sand. Dirty, stinkin sand. I'm not on holiday, if that's what you've heard. I ain't off on some jolly with the boys while you and your mother sit twiddlin your thumbs at home. I'm out here doin a job – a job that means you can carry on sittin readin your fuckin books all day without worrying about havin bits of you splashed all over the pavement.

Anyway, what I'm askin – and maybe you could give this letter to your mother when you're through readin it so she understands this too – is that you do me a little favour. Take your paint set and dig out the blue and the yellow, then snap 'em in half and chuck 'em away. Same goes for your crayons and pencils. You don't need 'em. And before you say anything about colourin in the sky, you can do it black. I'm up half the night at the moment anyway, so at least it'll be fuckin accurate.

We're movin out again in the mornin so I'm not sure when I'll get a chance to post this. Hopefully before I receive your next picture ha. Take care of yourself, son. Don't forget the push-ups.

* * *

They're coming for me.

At first I thought I was being paranoid – the cars parked opposite the house for weeks on end, the strangers standing a touch too close in lifts and public spaces. The CCTV cameras that seem to stir and twitch each time I walk into range. No, I would tell myself. It was nothing but a string of unlikely coincidences, an unholy trick of the light. One too many trashy thrillers perhaps, mixed with a lifelong flair for the theatrical. There are no bogeymen in the closet, no monsters under the bed.

And yet.

The strangers do *stand too close. The cameras do seem to shrug and whir a little too enthusiastically each time I wait for the bus or cut through the park, craning their robotic necks to trace and record my every move:*

Smile! You're on film.

And even now, as I sit and write this, a dark blue Volvo is parked across the road, its headlights dimmed, the driver hidden behind heavily tinted windows. Its engine softly murmuring, even though it's been stationary for days. And I know – I know *– that soon, very soon,* they *will grow tired of watching. And then a nondescript man in a nondescript office in another time zone somewhere will nod his head and tick a box and will pick up the telephone and simply say:*

Now.

And that three-letter word will echo around the world, relaying from tower to satellite, across the ocean and through the sky, until finally – instantly *– it will be heard in the earpiece of another nondescript man in a nondescript car across the road from my home.*

And on hearing that word he will put down his binoculars and kill the engine and make the short journey across the road and up two flights of stairs to my apartment. He will knock on my front door. And he will put a single, silenced bullet in the middle of my head. And then I will be just another box that's been ticked.

Permanently.

Not that you should feel too sorry for me. We must all of us live our lives knowing that our door will eventually knock, be it by a po-faced doctor or a professional hit man. Most of us don't even get the luxury of a prior warning. My grandmother was making pasta al forno when her front door knocked. My brother-in-law was driving his BMW.

No matter who you are – rich, poor, young, old – there's

an unwelcome caller out there somewhere who just won't take 'no' for an answer, who will hammer on your door until they finally get an answer. But what are you going to do? There's no sense in sitting and wishing your whole life away while you wait for the rap of knuckles unknown.

And so I refuse.

Instead I sit and I look around my sad little home, my memories nailed to the wall, faded but robust. In my bedroom above my writing desk I still have the flag from the first rally I attended, the lettering smudged but the message still as bold as it ever was:

Not In My Name.

It seems a long time ago now.

Yet even with the passage of time, with so much spilt sand – and blood – I can picture myself tossing aside the pins and unfurling it from the window. At least then the killer across the street would have something worth spying on for once. At least then he might stop, just for a second, and think of me not as a problem that needs solving, as a reaction that needs neutralising. As a steak that needs filleting. But as a living, breathing woman.

Wife.

Mother.

And, most importantly, somebody who is prepared to stand up and say:

No.

Whatever the consequences.

There's that flair for the theatrical I mentioned – though I promise you it's hard not to be a little hammy when you're facing the last few hours of your life. Especially when hanging on every wall and propped on every cabinet, sprinkled over bookshelves and piled on top of kitchen surfaces, there are little reminders of my time here on Earth. Artefacts that prove I existed, if only for a little while. A scale-model of the Eiffel Tower I picked up on a school trip to Europe, the ancient metallic paint flaking around the Champ de Mars; a not-so-

amusing fridge magnet designed to look exactly like a slice of Swiss cheese, a punch line, I think, to a long-forgotten joke.

And of course there are the photos. Everywhere the photos. Mum and Dad on their ten-year wedding anniversary; next to it a shot of Mum a few short years later, older, greyer. Infinitely sadder. There are photos of friends from so far back I hardly remember their names anymore, pictures of uncles and aunties at weddings and parties, my sister and my nieces grinning under mouse ears and ponchos, graduation photos, birthday photos… the milestones that together make up a life, frozen and framed, perma-sealed in perpetuity.

And then there are the photos I can't bear to look at. The ones whose absences are marked only by the lighter patches on my tired living room walls. A handsome young man in full military regalia; a bride wearing a smile even whiter and wider than her ridiculous puffball dress – images burnt so deeply on my heart that no amount of hiding will ever allow me to forget them. And yet I do hide them. Out of sight, out of mind, *as my poor mummy used to say, before she went irretrievably out of her own. Oh yes, I tuck them away and seal them up in boxes, these pictures I can't stand to see but am terrified of losing, along with all the others that I never quite got round to printing, lurking on hard drives and memory sticks in the darkest corners of my apartment, silicon ghosts rattling at the bottom of long-locked drawers.*

Yet of all these not-really-forgotten memories, there is one that stands out above the rest. It is a picture of a baby, curled foetal, his black and white smile preserved in nothing but sound.

It is a picture of a promise.

And for some reason, this is the picture I have dredged up from the depths of my secret boxes and propped before me on the desk tonight. And as I settle down to stare at it, this grainy copy I haven't looked at in half a year yet whose every pixel I know better than my own face, I suddenly begin to understand the reason why I have kept everything for so long.

It is because I have a story to tell.

And I must tell it tonight.

So that is why, even as death sits idling outside in a medium-sized family saloon, I am sat calmly at my desk with my boxes of exiled photos open around my feet and my laptop ready and loaded. Because just as I have been watched, I have been watching. I have been listening. Taking notes. Planning my story. And now, in lieu of anyone else who could conceivably save me, I'd like to tell it to you.

My son.

* * *

If you don't like walkin you might as well forget it. It ain't like the adverts, I can tell ya that for nothin. We don't come ridin in on no fleet of twinklin tanks. There ain't no charge of the light brigade ha. Not with the budget we're on. No choppers neither, not after deployment anyhows. They might buzz you in and swoop back down to scrape up what's left of you afterwards, but in between time it's just you and your hooves. You should see my feet, I'm serious. I got calluses tougher than a hunk of rump. Corns too – Christ, they're even uglier than your mother's trotters after a night on the tiles ha.

I ain't the worst off though. Nah. I met a guy a coupla weeks back I knew from basic trainin. Young lad, Schmitt or Schwarz or some other Kraut name you have to cough up a lung to pronounce. Nice kid. We'd been out in the field for days – *walkin* – when we land at a supply camp, someplace east of the Devil's Arsehole or somethin. That's where I see this Schmitt kid, hangin over by the tent with his unit. I figure I'll go over and say hi, see how the last few years been treatin him and whatnot, when I spot he's got one of his legs bandaged up. Don't look like there's much left but a stump.

Straightaway I start sweatin, thinking maybe he's seen some action. Seen one of *them*. I don't say nothin of course. I don't wanna swell the young man's head, so we jus' shoot the shit about nothing in particular, bitchin about some pin head colonel we both served under, catchin up on other guys from basic and whatnot, when out of nowhere he points down at his leg and gives the stump a little wiggle. 'Bet ya wondrin how I done this huh?' he says, all proud like, as if he were showin off the damn Victoria Cross or somethin. I shrug, playin it cool like I hadn't noticed. 'Some big fuckin mosquito getcha?' I laughed, diggin him in the ribs. The kid's face goes all serious, and for a second I think he's gonna say it. Gonna tell me how he's actually had a chance to go hand-to-hand with one of those bastards while I've spent the last six months marchin in circles like Donnie Dumbfuck. My stomach went cold and hard. 'Trench foot,' he says, and I started breathin again. Of course he ain't seen nothin. No one has.

'Trench foot!' I laugh. 'How the fuck you manage to get trench foot in the desert?' The kid looked down at his mangled leg, givin it another twitch for good measure before lookin up, a big stupid grin breakin out all over his face. 'Doc says it was me socks.' A couple of his boys turned around and laughed at this. 'Little prick never changed 'em. Kept squirtin his canteen down there too. Said it kept his feet cool,' one of them said. 'Ya feet nice and cool now huh?' We all laughed at that.

Anyhow, I ain't bitchin bout the walkin. There's just a whole lot of it is all. We walk. Yomp. Hump. March. Trek. Hike. Always with our shit tied to our backs like we're fuckin huskies or somethin. Pup tent, roll mat, sleepin bag, spare uniform, t-shirts, boots, spare socks – ha – hygiene kit, ration kit, medication, canteen and CamelBak, water, water, water, shovel, pick, knife, binoculars, compass, flashlight, gasmask, helmet, radio, grenades, assault rifle, ammo, ammo, ammo. And that's without all the other hi-tech crap they got us luggin around. That's the shit that really gets my goose. Y'know when I first joined up, way back whenever on Day One, they took us into a little room and played us this video. *Best of the*

Best of the Best, or somethin. It showed this group of lads bein parachuted in behind enemy lines, right in the dead of night. At first everythin's fine, they're crawling through the dirt on their bellies, when all of a sudden the shit hits the windmill. Explosions, gunfire – there's even a coupla them Doberman dogs yappin and snarlin after 'em. This one guy, the hero of the piece, reaches into his pack and all he's got is a plastic bag and a length of rope and few stale biscuits. Needless to say he manages to see off the enemy, save the day and earn himself a commendation, all before breakfast. The film ends with a tagline: *The Army – You Are the Weapon!*

Well what I want to know is this: if we're supposed to be the weapon then how comes we have to haul round all this robotic shit with us the whole time. GPS, night-vision goggles, laser sights, video cameras, e-mail. I got a radar in my helmet that can detect people hidin in a concrete bunker over 1000km away and a wrist-mounted display that I can watch porno videos on all night if I want to – both of them run off solar-powered fuel cells on my backpack. Yet in basic I learnt how to crack a guy's skull open using nothin but a stick. It jus' don't sit right. It's like it degrades us, the technology. Turns us into machines. Sometimes I wonder if it's there to assist us or if we're there to assist it.

Anyhow, that's why I like writin to ya son. Proper writin – scratchin on a pad with a rusty ol' nib. So you get somethin you can hold in your hands and keep, somethin ya can shove under your beak and take a sniff of and know you're smellin what I've been smellin. Dust and sweat and toil. Mind you, they're no good at gettin letters through this end. I think it's been six weeks since I got your last one. Which reminds me, there's a coupla questions from last time that I'm overdue answerin, so here they are:

What do you eat for breakfast?

Now that's an easy one. Ain't no Coco Pops or Weetabix neither. Nah. We got our MREs, see. Our *Meals Ready-to-Eat,* or *Meals Rejected by Everyone* as I like to call 'em ha.

Little brown packets of misery; freeze dried bacon and eggs or waffles and maple syrup or sausage and beans – all of it tastin more or less the same. Like wood shavings and dog shit. Only somehow less appealin. Now these things are scientifically engineered by the powers that be to balance nutritional requirements against portability and endurance. Apparently you could fire them in a rocket to the moon and they'd still be edible fifty years from now. And I do use the word edible lightly. So yeah, we got our MREs for breakfast, lunch and dinner, plus freeze dried coffee and dessert for afters. Just add water for instant satisfaction ha. Christ, we've even got little sachets of freeze dried water they make us carry round with us – go figure.

Have you killed anyone yet?

Well son, that's a funny one…

* * *

The biggest days of your life begin like any other. The morning you fall in love, the afternoon you find out you're pregnant. The evening the world ends. They all start the same way. Maybe it's the birds that wake you. Maybe the bin men. Whatever – the important thing to remember is that there will be no drum roll, no fireworks, no sign that your universe is about to be irrevocably rocked for richer or poorer, for better or worse.

There will be no four-minute warning.

And so on That Morning you do as you've always done. You open your eyes. You say hello to the world. *You get out of bed. You think about breakfast. You worry about what to wear. You fill your head and the air around you with urgent trivialities, all those non-conversations that on any other day would simply bounce off the walls and disappear into the ether. But not today. Because today is about to lurch so dramatically away from all of your expectations that months later – decades from now – you will still be waking in the middle of the night, straining to remember the tiniest, most-insignificant details of this otherwise ordinary morning to see if there was perhaps some sliver of a clue that would have given you an inkling of what was about to occur, some clumsy foreshadowing that you somehow managed to miss. The tap-tap-total obliteration of your father's teaspoon on an egg top; the breezy cadence of your mother's meteorological observations:*

It's going to be a hot one.

And of course, the deafening silence of all the things you forgot to say. That is what will keep you awake most often. That is what will hurt the most later on. Because you have no idea this will be your last chance to explain how blissfully happy you are at this precise blink in time, how thankful you are for this imperfectly perfect moment. And even if on some vague level you do understand that the status quo cannot be maintained indefinitely, that things will inevitably change, rupture – fall apart – you are too young to put these feelings into words. And so you just sit around and eat your Sugar Puffs and worry about your hair and talk and talk and talk.

And say nothing.

It was the alarm that woke me that morning, each of Mickey's malformed arms reaching for six. 'Oh boy! It's time to rise and shine!' *It was Friday, the last day before the summer break, and even as I lay groaning and opening my eyes and fumbling for the snooze button, I was remembering all of the fun that awaited me at school: the end of term party, the last chance to see my friends for six impossibly long weeks. The cakes! And so it was in a glitzy pink party dress rather than my usual regulation grey skirt and blazer that I descended the stairs and made my way to the kitchen table, where my older sister, mother and father were already busily buzzing, bobbing and weaving around each other, eating toast, ironing shirts, straightening ties, boiling and re-boiling the kettle, all of them with one eye on the clock.*

Tick-tock-tick-tock.

Looking back now, through the warped windows of tragedy and time, my tendency is to elevate that breakfast to almost mythical status, to see it as a picture perfect tableau of 1950's manners and domesticity. And nobody bickered or shouted or swore or spilt scalding coffee down their top. *But of course in reality we were just a regular family and it was just a regular breakfast. My sister sulked and Mum burnt the toast and Dad rushed from one end of the house to the other looking for his keys while the whole time I just went on and on and on about the stupid goddamned party until just about everybody felt like beating me around the head.*

Probably.

But one thing I do remember, and this isn't just pink-tinted historical revisionism, is that as just as the breakfast melee was nearing its inevitably messy climax – Mum sending yet more innocent slices of bread to the crematorium and giving up on breakfast altogether; my sister singeing her arm on the still-hot iron and recklessly howling four forbidden letters – Dad, already running perilously late for work, unexpectedly rushing back into the house and dazedly declaring: I forgot to say goodbye. *Before stooping to land a stubbly kiss on each of our cheeks.*

And then he was gone.

By the time I got to school it was already all over the playground, the hiss of hushed rumours like a punctured beach ball slowly deflating. Someone said the headmistress had been seen in tears. Somebody else mentioned the caretaker swearing loudly at the very top of his voice. Parents, their ears glued to blaring car radios, screeched to a halt outside the school gates only to bundle their children back into their cars mid-drop, while an ever-growing gaggle of sixth-formers congregated around the jungle gym, frantically relaying news from the screens of their mobile phones to the lower years gathered around them, the hiss becoming a roar as the phrase tragic accident *was replaced by* catastrophic attack. *And still nobody seemed to know exactly what had happened, the panic growing and growing until eventually our teacher shepherded us into the hall and announced in a shaking voice that the school was to be closed with immediate effect due to the morning's shocking 'events'.*

As for me – stupid, childish Lorna – I was more devastated by the cancellation of the end of term party than by the images and video footage that had begun to emerge, flashing up on billboards and shop windows as I sullenly made my way back home.

Videos of skyscrapers reduced to rubble.

Whole neighbourhoods engulfed in flames.

People screaming.

Blood.

Smoke.

It wasn't until I opened my front door and found my sister raw-eyed in front of the television that I started to realise that this was something big. Something bigger than I had vocabulary to digest. I sat down and started trying to follow the news footage, doing my best to grow up, *to* stop acting like such a baby. *But it was no good. No matter how hard I focused on the TV screen I couldn't seem to convince myself I was watching anything other than some cheesy monster-budget summer blockbuster; the CGI fireballs so obviously fake, the buildings tumbling in slow-motion, rewind and again, rewind and again. And then the picture switched to a LIVE report and I started to recognise the neighbourhood, an intrepid female reporter ducking under police tape and battling dust and flames to show the blackened remains of an office block in the city centre.*

Dad's office.

And just like a movie the phone started screeching and my sister got up without a word. I reached for the remote and tried to switch over but it was no good, the news was on every channel, the reporter's brow expertly furrowed as she approached my father's place of work, the doorway charred and gaping like a mouthful of rotten teeth.

My sister picked up the phone and said hello.

The police were trying to turn the reporter back, telling her it wasn't safe to be there. But she didn't care and instead started moving round the side of the building, the camera panning up towards the burnt-out windows, flames still licking out from the demolished panes.

My sister put down the phone.

The reporter was shaking her head and clutching her earpiece. Her editor was speaking to her, right now, LIVE on-air and she was relaying the information.

No survivors.

Rewind and again.

My sister started screaming.

And at that moment I finally understood what was happening, what all of this meant. It meant I didn't need to worry about acting like a baby anymore. It meant I wouldn't act like a baby ever again. Because as the news reporter signed off with a grim nod and my sister's face dissolved into a torrent of snot and tears, I felt something harden inside me, deep beneath my stupid pink party dress. There was no time for crying, I realised, for maudlin self-pity. Because it was about survival now.

About Us versus Them.

We were under attack.

I was twelve years old.

* * *

Son if anyone ever asks ya if ya want the good news or the bad news first, save yourself a whole world of bother and shoot them in the fuckin face right then and there. I'm serious. Whenever someone asks you a question like that, ya know for a fact that there ain't no good news at all – they're just sprinklin a spoonful of sugar on a shovelful of shit. And boy, did I get a shovel of shit flung my direction this mornin. More like a whole fuckin cartload, I'd say. And believe me, it's gonna take a whole lot more than soap and water to get the stink out. A whole lot more.

We reached the F.O.B. – our Forward Operating Base – early yesterday evening. Even though I must've been here a half-dozen times over the last two years, I still never get over the size of the place. It's like an entire city they've built out here in the desert; shops, hospitals, cinemas, chapels, mosques, temples – a fuckin Pizza Hut – bars and a prison (which is normally full of good ol' boys who've had one too many in the bars ha), all of it linked by real, honest-to-goodness gravel roads. In fact it's only when ya get up close ya notice that all the buildings are either giant tents or breeze block, with sheets of corrugated roofing angled this and thataway, like a shantytown or somethin. There's impermanence to the place, as if it was thrown up overnight. Looks like it could be torn down jus' as quickly too.

Anyhow as soon as we got in I hit the barracks for the three S's – a shower, a shit and a shave. Ya don't know what it is to take a dump in a real toilet until you've spent twelve weeks squatting over a hole you've dug in the dirt. Feels like sittin on a goddamned throne when you first get on there, like you're the Queen of England or somethin. Once I'd finished I met up with a couple of the guys from my unit and got to drinkin. Like I said, they've got a few bars set up for us to blow off steam. They even got a girly show down here, some big-tittied southern piece shootin ping-pong balls out her whatsit. Real trashy like – I half wondered if she might know your mother, ha.

For whatever reason though, none of us really enjoyed it as much as we was pretendin to, so mostly we jus' ignored the poontang and stuck to the drinkin. Christ, we musta put away nearly a case of bourbon between us. The good stuff too. Imported. Still, it was quiet for a first night back at base. For once the liquor never really got to us. If anythin it made us quieter, morose even, each of us sat there mullin our thoughts, thinkin about the meetin in the mornin.

Thinkin about war.

At around a half past one I decided enough was enough and cut out. Halfway back to the barracks though, I changed my mind and took a trip out to the shootin range instead. Now sometimes the safety officers can get a little pissy when they know you've had a few, but and as luck would have it I recognised the guy on the desk from my first tour – Harry somethin-or-other, from 35th – and after chewin my ear for ten minutes he signed me out a semi-automatic and waved me through. I picked a lane at the far end of the range, slipped on my goggles and ear defenders and started blastin away.

It sounds funny, but as a soldier I don't get to fire off a weapon nearly as often as I'd like. From the pictures they show on TV, you'd think we spend pretty much every other day shootin at bad guys and blowin up shit. The truth is the only time I ever really get to let off a few rounds is out on the range.

Unless I'm shootin up goat herders that is ha.

But seriously, out in the desert they've got every fuckin bullet numbered and accounted for. All that health and safety and bureaucracy and whatnot, it fucks up every good thing left in the world. I mean, we've even had memos reminding us to consider the financial burden of ammunition. I'm not kiddin! Apparently we're supposed to think before we shoot now to see whether the money could be better spent buldin an orphanage for dune-coons or somethin – like the price of bullets is gonna enter your head when you're lying in a puddle of your best friend's blood, surrounded by you-know-whats. Like you can put a cost on a life.

But I guess that's politicians for ya – rich fucks who've never seen a day's service in their lives. I swear to god one of these days someone's gonna send 'em a wakeup call they'll never forget. We'll see if they're still considerin the financial burden of ammunition when they're staring down the wrong end of a barrel.

I don't know how long I stayed there, firin expensive

bullets at cheap card targets, but by the time I finished up it was almost light, the sky that special bruised-eye purple that you only get out here in the desert. I looked around for Harry but his desk was empty. I guessed his shift was finished, but there was no sign of a replacement safety officer, which kinda pissed me off to be honest. I mean, I ain't much one for paperwork but still, there had to be at least a coupla hundred grand's worth of fireworks locked up behind that two-bit safe. I'd hate to think what could happen if the wrong person got in there. We'd be in for a right ol' show, ha.

Anyhow, I wasn't interested in landin Harry in the shit, so I signed the gun back in myself and started on the walk back to the barracks, figurin I'd get myself a shower and freshen up before the meetin. I wasn't sleepy at all by that point, and it felt pretty good to be out alone in the early mornin air with my boots pressin into that proper road beneath me, the endless sky bleedin pink and red over east. You ever watched the sun rise in the desert son? Don't matter how many times I seen it, it always manages to catch me off guard. The speed of it. And the colours, Jesus. It's like you're bearin witness to somethin holy. The birth of the day my ol' man used to call it – that big ball of flame like a baby's head crownin, cleavin the sky in two. It's somethin to see, I'll tell ya that for nothin. It's somethin to see.

By the time I got back onto the main drag the world had begun to stir, people scuttlin like bugs, puttin up banners, assemblin a makeshift stage in the middle of the street, ready for Commander Big Bollocks to give his speech. I nodded to a few guys I recognised but most were too busy to wave back, draggin things from one side of the road to the other, puttin up and takin down scaffoldin, fiddlin with electrical cable and lightin rigs. It was great to watch actually, everyone workin together like that, back-to-back, shoulder-to-shoulder. Like a machine. Nobody complainin or mitherin or questionin nothing. Jus' followin orders until the job was done. It's the way any good army has to be – whether you're puttin up a stage or flattenin a village – and standin there, bathed in the warmth of the new day while I watched my buddies work, well I don't mind tellin you that the whole fuckin world looked golden. Of course, I didn't know then how badly I was about to get fucked over.

A coupla hours later I was sat with my platoon on a fold-out steel chair, about forty rows back from the stage. There must've been twenty thousand of us there, sweatin our backsides off in full uniform, slowly losin the will to live. There'd been a couple of delays already – technical hitches with the sound, plus what felt like months of administrative bullshit – and by the time Commander BB finally took to the stage we near enough fuckin evaporated with relief, whoopin and hoopin so loud that our Lieutenant had to stand up and tell us to simmer down. Big Bollocks though, he jus' lapped it up, standin there with his hands in the air like he were the goddamned Holy Pope absolvin us of our fuckin sins or somethin. He must've stood there like that for a whole five minutes before he finally stepped forward to the microphone and gave a triumphant: 'Hell yeah!'

Well that started us off all over again, and we spent another five minutes whistlin and hollerin before he raised his hands to address us properly. 'Men… and ladies.' We had a good laugh at that. Whilst the brochures would have you believe that the modern army is some sort of omni-gendered-multi-cultural-homo-lovin-rainbow-tribe, the reality is that women only make up about ten or eleven percent of the entire forces, and out here in the desert that number drops to virtually nil, other than the cooks, cleaners and dancin girls, plus a handful of wasp chompin bull-dykes who you wouldn't fuck with your worst enemy's dick ha.

After the laughter died down, the Commander continued. 'As I'm sure you're all aware, next January will represent the eleventh anniversary of our invasion and, well I don't know how to say this other than… We. Are. Winning!' Well the whole fuckin place jus' went off – men up off their seats chest bumpin, Mexican wavin, a fuckin carnival dancin all around me. Course Big Bollocks carried on milkin it for a while, roarin like some sheriff from the old west, his carefully scripted asides like cubes of steak to a pack of starvin dogs. 'Those scum suckin sons of bitches are on the back foot! We're kickin their asses!' he yelled, on and on and on.

Eventually, when the men had been whipped up to a rapturous climax not even our lieutenants could silence, the Commander once again raised his hands in the air and appealed for silence. 'Now, I've got some good news and some bad news…' He paused, leaning forward slightly and gesturing to someone off-stage. Immediately a large projection sprang up on a screen behind him, a familiar artist's impression of the enemy leader; a snarlin, six-armed son-of-a-bitch towerin over a pile of eviscerated human torsos, a string of black drool hangin from a thousand serrated teeth, a single red eye planted in the middle of his ugly fuckin forehead – maybe you've seen him before? I think they used a model of him on one of the high school promotional drives a way back. Sort of looks like your mother first thing in the mornin ha.

Anyway, the crowd instinctively started up with the jeerin and booin, even the lieutenants joinin in now, even me, while Big Bollocks stood quietly on the stage, his entire body seeming to pulsate with disgust. 'Makes you wanna puke, don't it? But the sad fact is that he, and hundreds more like him, are still out there, roaming the desert, probing for weaknesses, plotting our ultimate destruction. We might be winning the war… but the war is still a long way from won.' He paused for effect, starin gravely out at us, before he allowed his face to soften slightly, raising an eyebrow, a crooked grin pullin at the corner of his lips. 'That's the bad news!' A light ripple of laughter broke out. Gee, the Commander sure was a card. Yee-ha! He knew how to work the crowd alright, how to push our buttons. What a guy! Big Bollocks paused again, savourin the moment, his smile broadenin, showin almost as many teeth as the guy in the picture. 'Now for the good news... '

We waited, our breaths held, our bodies tinglin with anticipation. Because this was the moment we'd been waiting for. Our wise and charismatic leader was about to give the word, and by Christ we were ready! Ready to attack, to kill, to win – ready for war!

'... You're all going home!'

The silence that followed was the purest I've ever known. Nobody rattled their chairs or stamped their boots or cleared their throats or scratched their stubble. I could hear the blood hissin in my ears, as if I were deflatin, the air leakin outta me. And then the world exploded, not in anger or protest, but in fuckin jubilation. The bastards were actually dancin – clappin their hands, cheerin in delight. They were pleased to be going home. Me, I sat there numb. The Commander continued for another half hour or so, outlining the role of drones in the new strategy, emphasisin the fact this was a withdrawal and not a retreat. Eventually he passed over to a junior who briefed us on the logistical details. Apparently the withdrawal was to be staggered over the next six months, with the longest servin platoon to be shipped home first. Meanin I'm at the front of the queue, whoop-de-fuckin-doo.

The junior drawled on for a bit longer, explainin that for whatever reason the jump off point was an airstrip 100km to the north, which, naturally, we'd have to make our way to on foot. Then they wheeled Big Bollocks out one last time so he could pump his fist in the air again and call us all heroes and a credit to our country and promise us all medals when we got home. And then the meetin was over and they played the anthem and everyone stood up and clapped and cheered as we filed back to our barracks to pack up our things. Which is what I'm doin now.

So son, it looks like you'll be seein me sooner than expected, not in five months but in five days. That's the 'good news'. In other words I'm bein made unemployed, sneakin off home like Larry Limp-dick to leave a bunch of toy planes to mop up what the politicians are too tight-fisted to finish.

But that was never the deal.

We got into this knowin it was grimy, horrible, back-breakin work; we knew it and we still jumped to sign on the dotted line. Couldn't get over here quick enough. Because there's a job to do out here. Monsters to kill. And jus' because nobody's happened to have seen 'em lately don't make 'em any less real. Any less deadly. And the thing is they're out there right now, son. I can feel 'em. Jaws open, arms wide, jus' waitin for us to slip up and turn our backs. To shrug our shoulders and stop believin. To go home. And when we do… ?

Well, sleep tight son.

* * *

There were rumours of course. There had always been rumours. A field of mutilated sheep, a few kids missing on the same street – people loved to talk. But deep down everyone knew they were just stories. An attempt to explain the unexplainable, to make some sense of the merciless world. A bit of barstool banter for half-cut grown-ups, a chance to scare over-imaginative kids. Either that, or they were there to warn us; a handy metaphor used by filmmakers and storytellers to stand in for whatever evil they were keen to explore – cancer, Communists, consumerism. A clumsy parable designed to make us

Stop.

Think.

And then carry on.

Even when the stories leaked from the playgrounds and factory floors to the TVs and newsstands – vague intelligence alluding to dark plots or sinister forces, a journalist beheaded in some made-up country we could hardly pronounce – they were met with scepticism, or more commonly indifference. The pictures were always a little too blurry. The timing of each leak a touch too convenient. And so they were relegated to supermarket tabloids and daytime TV; titillation to sprinkle between the heaving cleavages and freak diet tips at the end of the checkout. Something to shift copy. There was no way any intelligent adult – or even a reasonably bright twelve-year-old girl for that matter – would react with anything other than a shake of the head and a knowing smile whenever they heard the word:

Monsters.

But then one day we woke up and found out they weren't stories any more. There was fire in the air and bodies in the street and twenty-four hour looped news coverage to prove it. Apparently provoked by little more than our on-going existence, Monsters had launched a surprise attack on the capital city – my city *– killing hundreds and leaving thousands more injured and disfigured.*

My father was dead and the streets were burning.

Nothing would ever be the same again.

To say the summer that followed the attack was a wash-out would be to do a grave injustice to wash-outs the world over. For the first few weeks we all made a super-human effort at maintaining normality, especially Mum. After getting over her initial shock, our mother went into ultra-pragmatic mode. Her cubs were in danger. Her job was to protect and nourish. To help us move on. Or at least to provide suitable distractions from our grief.

Therefore, two days after the attack I woke to the noxious choke of fresh paint, and I emerged onto the landing to find Mum clad in white overalls, roller in hand, having apparently decided to redecorate the entire upstairs of our house. This was after she had already sorted and bagged all of Dad's clothes, leaving them neatly lined up beside the door of a charity shop. I didn't see her cry once during those first couple of weeks and, while we were not exactly barred from doing so, I got the impression that any show of emotion would be distinctly inappropriate. After all, this was officially a National Tragedy – *the President had called it a 'State of Emergency'. We were all in this together.*

Except.

As the weeks wore on and the new reality of our splintered family began to hit home, it was difficult to imagine feeling less alone. Once the funeral was out of the way (Dad's body was never recovered so we ended up burying an empty wooden box), Mum began to lose focus, and in the same amount of time it had taken for the Tributes to the Fallen to slip from the front page to a small box on page thirty-seven, Mum found herself running out of DIY projects to undertake. Or rather, she ran out of the motivation to finish them – leaving behind her a trail of half-painted walls, exposed floorboards and unassembled wardrobes. Instead she began to fold under the weight of despair, spending more and more time in bed on a diet of made-for-TV melodramas and repeat prescription tranquilisers. My sister, already sixteen at the time, quickly abandoned us for the relative stability of her boyfriend's house, leaving me to single-handedly navigate our fast-sinking family ship. Naturally, things quickly spiralled out of control.

Post lay stacked on the mat, bills unopened, unpaid. Milk curdled in glasses on the living room floor and plates stacked up on the side, festering, unwashed, as I took to eating straight from the tin, carton, tub or whatever I could scavenge from our rapidly dwindling supplies. Some days I ate nothing but peanut butter and processed cheese. Others I would snack on cold soup and bacon sprinkles.

As far as I could tell, Mum didn't eat anything at all.

The worst thing was the lack of escape. Living centrally, most of my friends had lost at least one family member in the attack, and it was as if a suffocating mourning shroud had been draped across my entire neighbourhood. The bowling alley, swimming pool, arcade and ice cream parlour had all closed their doors as a mark of respect, and even the parks and public squares remained resolutely deserted. For all intents and purposes summer was cancelled, leaving me with little to do but skulk around the house, trying hopelessly to avoid the reminders of my normal life that had ended with a roar only a few weeks earlier. So I did what any grieving not-quite-adolescent with time on their hands and no discernible parental guidance would do – I tapped into Dad's liquor cabinet (one of the few remaining souvenirs of Dad's time on Earth that Mum hadn't boxed up and shipped off to the oh-so-poor and needy), poured myself a glass of foul tasting single-malt and switched on the TV.

I tuned in.

Dropped out.

And so that summer, instead of heading to the beach or enjoying pyjama parties with my friends, I got loaded on premium brand spirits and, seeing as the news channels remained about the only things left on air worth watching, began taking an almost unnatural interest in World Affairs. And boy did I learn some interesting facts, sprawled out half-cut on our filthy sofa while Mum lay wasting away upstairs. For instance, in my previous incarnation as a bubbly, talkative, pop music-obsessed twelve-year-old girl I'd had no idea that only a short few thousand miles away across the sea there was an entire nation full of hideous, bloodthirsty Monsters just baying to tear us limb from limb. Now these freaks weren't people in the conventional sense, but deformed savages; things, *who despised us for our wholesomeness and democracy and prayed daily to their heathen gods for nothing short of our total annihilation. And that wasn't all. Not content with lone acts of Monsterism abroad – no matter how spectacular the results – these repulsive beasts were also responsible for the enslavement and subjugation of their own people; the rightful* indigenous *inhabitants of the sandy, faraway places where they lived. They were nothing but a cowardly bunch of bandits and butchers. Marauding murderers.*

And they had to be stopped.

One evening as I sat watching TV, a potent mix of expensive alcohol and political rhetoric coursing through my bloodstream, I suddenly found myself crying. Dabbing at my eyes with the edge of my week-old cardigan, I realised it wasn't despair that had caused me to spill out over the edges, or even the Stolichnaya vodka I'd mixed thickly with blackcurrant cordial, but something altogether more unfamiliar and surprising. I was crying with hope. Because as the images of repressed villagers flashed up on the screen – each of them as miserable and wretched as the survivors in my own home town – I could finally see with clarity the entire story in primary colours, as simple as any fairy-tale: There were goodies and baddies. Dark and light. On one side stood me, my mum, my sister, my dad, the government and all of the poor oppressed people around the world. On the other side: the Monsters. Suddenly I had a narrative thread to seize on, something to root for, an enemy to despise, to boo and hiss. It was a bit like supporting a football team.

And even as I blew my nose and smudged my eyes and basked in this glorious revelation, the news report just kept wheeling on, the presenter looking even more breathless and excited than usual as he touched his ear and informed us that... sorry, news just coming in and... we are interrupting this broadcast for a very special announcement from...

The President himself.

And there he was, right in my living room, his face as grey and sombre as his suit, his eyes moist with emotion and auto-cue eyestrain. In a serious voice he explained all about the two or three distant countries that were sheltering these Monsters – a Pivot of Poison *he called it – listing all of the terrible things the Monsters had done to the people who lived there, and what they would do to us if they ever got a chance. He used words like justice, safety and peace. All I heard was:*

Revenge.

The President went on, loosening his tie, leaning forward, talking directly to me. 'So what are we going to do about it, Lorna?' he asked. 'Are we going to let these bastards get away with murder?' I shook my head, longing for the words I knew he was about to say. 'Of course we ain't!' The president was all winks and smiles now, his accent growing stronger by the second. He was one of us *after all, just as sickened and tired by the whole sorry story as every other right-thinking, god-fearing patriot.*

And he weren't gonna take this sheet lyin' down!

'Now, I have hard, tangible intelligence that these scum-buckets are capable of launching an attack within five minutes of someone giving the order. Five minutes! *That's hardly enough time for a mother to tuck up her sweet innocent baby in bed and kiss them goodnight... ' The President paused for a moment to wallow in this image before stepping out from behind his lectern to welcome some Very Special Guests to the stage, the camera pulling back to reveal a host of world leaders, all nodding solemnly as the President resumed his speech. 'That is why I am pleased to announce that, along with my coalition here, we have decided to commence with immediate effect a sustained and intense military operation in order to free all people currently oppressed by these Monsters and protect the world from this grave and imminent danger... '*

There was a rapturous round of applause. Or at least there was in my head. And I imagine there was in living rooms around the world too. Of course there was! Because the good guys were coming to the rescue. Daddy might be dead and Mummy might be mad and I might be dizzyingly, deliriously drunk, but none of that mattered. The world was safe again. The city would be re-built, better, stronger than before. Things could only get better.

And even as the President was wrapping up his address, promising a swift and decisive victory, calling on God to bless all the selfless heroes who were putting their lives on the line for our country – for freedom – I was tearing myself away from the screen, racing up the stairs to shake Mother from her pharmaceutical slumber to tell her the good news: We were going to war.

* * *

You'll never believe how much blood there is in a human body until you've scraped the insides of your buddy from the front of your shirt.

There was an accident last night, son. Or at least an incident. Because from where I'm sittin, huddled in the dirty dawn light, it don't look like no accident. Nah. In fact it looks a whole lot like someone – or more likely somethin – did this on purpose. And what they've left behind, Jesus. Let's jus' say I hope you get this letter after breakfast.

I'll paint you a picture: Of the thirty-four men who set out two days ago, you can now count those left on the fingers of one hand. The rest of 'em are lyin in piles, stacked like meat in a butcher's truck. Bellies slit open, guts dangling in the dirt. Filleted. Steve, our medic, is lyin at my feet. His lungs are hangin from a tree a little down the path. This is the same Steve who nine hours ago was tellin me how he was gonna open up a little mechanics yard with his brother when he got home. The same Steve who'd jus' found out he had a little baby on the way, who was savin up for a bigger place, who was finally gonna pop the question to his girl. Lookin down at him now, I notice he's missin one of his eyes. Jus' clean plucked from his skull, the hollow socket starin back at me. Yup, I guess you could say that Steve's had a hell of a night one way or another. A hell of a night.

We'd got off to an early start. This was two days ago, the morning after Big Bollocks gave his song and dance on the stage. I hadn't slept again, and when the Staff Sergeant burst in at 0430 and started yellin I was stood washed and shaved with my roll packed. By the time the sun finally decided to show its lazy ass we'd already covered twenty kilometres. The guys were all in high spirits, listin off all the things they was gonna do when they got home, singin stupid songs and clownin around. Even the Lieutenant seemed relaxed, jokin with the men, turnin a blind eye to us smokin and whatnot. I was rostered as point man, which to be honest suited me jus' fine. I was happy to be out at the front of the pack and away from the rest of those fuckers. Anyway, bein on point out here ain't exactly what you'd call a challenge. The terrain is so flat you'd spot anythin approachin at least an hour away. As long as you keep one eye on the horizon all ya have to do is plod one foot in front of the other and zone out to the creep of your shadow across the sand. Besides, there ain't been any attacks out here for months now, years probably.

Up until last night that is.

About an hour before the sun went down we stopped to set up camp. Like I said it was a real party atmosphere, and while the Lieutenant stopped short at passin round a bottle of Jack, there were extra rations and whatnot. Ok, so the food still tasted like shit, but it was a nice gesture at least. After that it was business as usual, the night patrol team settin up a watch on the perimeter, the rest of the guys sleepin in shifts, me not sleepin at all. As usual I'd volunteered to swap with one of the boys halfway through the night, but after a coupla hours starin at the ceiling of my tent I got bored and decided to relieve him early.

Outside was colder than normal, and that's sayin somethin. It might be hotter than the burnin pits of hell durin the day here, but at night it drops colder than an eskimo's nut sack. I seen boys lose the tips of their fingers in a bad winter. Frostbite in the desert, son – how'd ya like that? Anyhow, I kept it nice and brisk as I made my way towards the perimeter, rubbin my hands together to keep warm until I hit the curtain of darkness that was draped round the camp. Then I was forced to stop rubbin and take out my torch. That's somethin else no one tells you about the desert. The darkness. On a moonless night there ain't nothin like it. I'm talkin blacker than pitch black, son. It's absolute – like you've been swallowed up or somethin. Your eyes don't adjust to it neither. I'm tellin ya, a man spends too much time in the dark, he gets to seein things. Only out here, you can't be 100% sure that the things you've seen ain't real.

The night boy, a young private named Cal, was real jumpy when I showed up, waving his rifle around until he clocked my uniform and stood to attention. Between you, me and the fencepost, I reckon he'd been havin forty winks on the sly, what with his puffy eyes and drool crusted face. Or maybe he was jus' a bit special. Either way, he settled down once I'd explained the situation to him and seemed pleased to be knockin off early. I watched him totter off towards the distant glow of the camp, suddenly filled with a sense of pride as I looked over at the small cluster of lights. Because that light stands for something, son – hope, righteousness, whatever. Lookin in from the dark, it felt like I was starin at a base on the moon or something; a tiny enclave of good set amongst the endless wickedness of the universe.

After a while though I noticed some of the tents were lit up, illuminated by the unmistakable flutter of LCD screens. I felt sick then, as I thought of my fellow soldiers – the most elite force of Monster-killers ever assembled – hunched over their roll mats watchin porno. Right then the little circle of light stopped lookin like a moonbase and started lookin like a zoo; nothing but a pack of gruntin animals whackin off 'til they was raw. I turned back to my post in disgust and stared out, the darkness lookin blacker than ever.

The next morning we set off before sunrise. This is yesterday. People were still upbeat, but by now the celebrations were more muted – the reality of spendin two more days trudgin through the desert startin to sink in. Once again I offered to take up the point and spent most of the day by myself, happy enough for some peace and quiet, just me and my thoughts. As before, we stopped about an hour before sunset, settin up camp in a small natural basin that offered a little shelter from the harsh wind that had started up as the afternoon'd wore on. There were no extra rations this time, and although we ate together there was little conversation, our backs, legs and feet achin from two days on the beat. I was jus' finishin up when Steve came over and started blabbin to me, goin on about his baby girl and whatnot. Even though I was only half listenin, he seemed real happy. I guess that's something, huh? After dinner the night patrol took up their posts while the rest of us hit the sack, and once again I found myself starin at the inside of my tent, unable to sleep. Just before midnight I gave up and figured I'd take another stroll out to the perimeter and see if I could swap with one of the night boys. No point in us both sittin up doin nothin all night.

As I crept out of the camp and into the darkness, I was struck by how quiet the night was. Now obviously compared to the city, the desert is always pretty quiet. Ya don't get much late night traffic passin through these parts ha. Still, after a few weeks out here you start to notice it ain't *that* quiet. Much like anywhere else, the desert has its own soundtrack, a heartbeat. A pulse. There's the wind of course, rustlin the shrubs and cacti, howlin through the caves and creeks. But there's life too – more than you'd expect considerin how downright inhospitable this cunt-crack of a country is. There's the squawk and chatter of birds in the mornin, desert larks mostly, though you might see the odd raven too, maybe even an eagle if you're lucky. Then as soon as the sun starts to dip a chorus of crickets clears its throat, with the occasional screech of frog punctuatin the song, though god knows where the little bastards manage to find water. There's bats too, squeakin and swoopin overhead, and the scratch and scurry of assorted rodents around your feet, all of it cemented together by the whine of mosquitoes and flies, which follow you round pretty much 24-7. Of the two, the flies are the worst, the lack of moisture out here drivin 'em gaga, so that you spend every other second swattin 'em outta your nose, mouth and eyeballs while they're tryna suck the juice outta ya. There's bigger things out here too; wild pigs, cattle, badgers even. And then there's the things you can't name, odd rustles and grunts you don't recognise. The scratch of unfamiliar claws on sand, distant screams in the night. It's enough to give you nightmares. Well it would be, if I could ever get any goddamned sleep that is, ha.

Last night though, the desert was quiet. I mean fuckin silent. No crickets, mosquitoes, nothin. Even the wind had dropped away, and as I approached the edge of the basin the crunch of my footsteps echoed loud and crisp in the cold night air. The noise must've given me away to the night boy, and as I approached I saw that it was that Cal kid, wavin his torch and gun around like he was the damn Lone Ranger or somethin. The dumb shit'd probably been sleepin on the job again. 'Evenin Sir,' he said, droppin the rifle and salutin as soon as he made me out in the dark. I looked him up and down, his shiny pink face rigid with concentration. A teenager. Tell the truth he didn't look much older than you son – I'd put money on his balls bein just as smooth too, ha.

'Give the 'Sir' shit a rest, Private,' I said, tossin him a box a smokes. The kid nodded to me, relaxin as he took out a cigarette and lit up. 'Couldn't sleep again, huh?' he asked, handing me back the box. 'Not as well as you,' I shot back. The kid blinked a couple of times, a look of panic flushin his face like he knew he'd been caught out. 'Ah relax, son. I'm jus' breakin ya balls. I thought I'd swing by and let you bunk off early again. Seein as it's such a lovely night and all.' We laughed at that, the shadows of our cigarettes unspoolin in the torch light. Then the kid thanked me and set off towards camp, the orange glow from his smoke like a sniper's sight in the dark.

At first I thought it was thunder, which is ridiculous, I know. As if a soldier wouldn't recognise the sound of automatic rifle fire when he heard it. I guess it jus' caught me by surprise is all, the short bursts seemin to come from nowhere, rattlin around the basin like rolls on a snare. RATA-TATA-TATA.

Pause. RATA-TATA-TATA. Sounded like a whole fuckin marchin band down there I'm tellin ya. It wasn't until I heard a grenade explode that my brain finally caught up and my training kicked in, muscle memory eclipsin fear as I started to sprint.

When I was a coupla minutes from camp the gunfire abruptly cut away, jus' leavin the sound of me puffin and pantin as I entered the camp. There was blood everywhere – I mean EVERYWHERE – the circle of green tents decorated with dark crimson arcs, the sand still wet to the touch. 'Hello?' I called, raising my rifle to my chest. There was no response. As quietly as I could, I crept over to the Lieutenant's tent. Sure enough I found him face down on his mat, little pieces of his skull splattered across the canvas.

As I backed away from the mess I heard a loud noise behind me, and I dived for cover, letting off a loud burst of warnin fire as I hit the dirt. 'HOLD FIRE!' someone called, our Staff Sergeant Jim staggerin towards me wavin his hands, two others close behind. 'That you, Corporal?' he asked, as the smoke cleared. 'Yes Sir. What the hell's happened here Sir?' Jim took a step forward, shrugging his shoulders. 'Fucked if I know. I was out on the west perimeter when I heard gunfire.' He paused a second, 'You hurt soldier?' I followed his gaze to my chest, finding the front of my jacket smeared red. 'The Lieutenant,' I explained, wiping at my top. 'Who you got with you?' Jim nodded at the two soldiers behind him. 'Corporal Doggerel and Private Jettison,' he replied. 'They were together over on the north point. We found Steve round the back there. I ain't sure where the rest of him is… '

A loud crash interrupted him and we turned to see Doggie and Jett sprintin out towards the edge of the camp, returnin a few seconds later with a wrigglin pink thing pinned between them. 'Cal!' I shouted, recognisin the kid I'd relieved an hour earlier, except now he was wearing nothing but his underwear and was screamin his head off. 'THEY'RE GONNA KILL US MAN! WE NEED TO GET OUT OF HERE!' As they brought him closer I saw he weren't fakin it, his eyes buggin out his head. 'Stand to attention Private!' Jim hollered, and the kid seemed to relax a bit then, instinct takin over as he started saluting over and over like a robot while he stood shiverin in his boxer shorts. 'Now in your own words Private, can you explain what in fuck's name's been happenin round here.' The kid looked at Jim, then at the two guys holdin him, and then over at me. And then, without a word, we watched as a dark stream of piss trickled down his bare leg and soaked into the sand below.

We got Cal talkin in the end of course, though it turned out he knew as little as the rest of us. He was half way back to camp when he heard the first shots. He started runnin and didn't look back. When he got back everyone was dead. We let him get dressed while the rest of us searched for survivors, stackin the bodies we found in piles to make 'em easier to count. I gave up lookin once I'd counted twenty, but Jim, Doggie and Jett carried on searchin, emptyin tents, shakin out bloodied sleepin bags. Well good on 'em I say. Me, I decided to have a little sit down. I'd seen enough blood for one night.

About a half hour ago Jim came over and dumped Steve's body at my feet, his chest cavity flappin open as he hit the floor. 'That's 'em all,' he said, pointedly. I shrugged, lit another cig. Jim told me they'd conducted a full search of the site, and nearly all of our equipment had either been destroyed or pillaged in the raid, along with the majority of our food and water supplies. 'You got somethin to say about that, Corporal?' I shook my head, suckin up my smoke. It was almost daybreak, the sky turned a sickly white. Jim looked like shit. 'You got somethin to say?' he asked again, and once again I shook my head. From where I was sittin the campsite looked like an impressionist painting or somethin, the flattened tents like lily pads on a lake of sand and blood. It didn't seem like it'd make much difference whether I had anythin to say or not. A sudden commotion on the other side of the camp interrupted us, as Cal burst from his tent, his shirt on back-to-front, screamin his head off again.

'AHHHHH! WE'RE FUCKED! WE'RE TOTALLY FUCKED!'

Jim shot me one last look before runnin off to join Doggie and Jett, who by now'd already tackled Cal to the floor. As I watched them restrain the poor little prick, twistin his arm up behind his back and pushin his face in the dirt, I couldn't help thinkin:

The kid had a point.

* * *

There had been protests at first. Marches and rallies took place in the streets while politicians squabbled over the finer details of the invasion: Exactly which countries were harbouring Monsters? And how quickly were they capable of launching another attack? Forty-five minutes? Forty-five days? In the end though it all proved to be academic. Within weeks war was everywhere, as much a part of the national conversation as global warming and mass unemployment. In other words, it was boring – simply another voice adding to the vaguely depressing background babble, which tried and failed to compete with the other, far more urgent, concerns of the general public. Namely reality television and the consumption of vast and destructive quantities of alcohol.

Naturally, I was far more interested in the latter.

I was in my final year of college, approaching my finals – a miraculous position to find myself in considering the years I'd spent binging. I'm not just talking about booze either. In the intervening years since the attack (which the press had snappily branded Year Zero*) I'd found any number of anaesthetics to keep me distracted: sex, pot, pills, poetry – I even got into religion for a few months following an ill-fated crush on a Jewish boy when I was sixteen – but none of it had really stuck. No, the only constant companion I'd had on* *my journey from youth to young womanhood was drink. Not usually to the point of incapacitation – just enough to soften the harsher edges of reality, to blur the details.*

To numb the memories.

I don't know whether I'd describe myself as an alcoholic exactly. If I was then I was high-functioning – probably a little too high-functioning for my liking, as I found no matter how drunk I was I could never really escape the mental shadow cast by my sad little family. And believe me, they were sad. Having permanently fled to the sanctuary of her boyfriend's house, my sister initially seemed to have emerged from the carnage relatively unscathed, graduating from law school with good grades before immediately taking a job down south, about as far away from Mum – and from me – as she could get without falling into the sea. For the next five years or so she led an unexpectedly happy life; keeping a good job, getting married and giving birth to an adorable set of twin girls. During this period I visited my sister a total of three times, on each occasion getting the distinct impression she would rather I wasn't there. Whenever I did speak to her, she went out of her way not to ask after Mum. She couldn't even bring herself to say Dad's name.

One morning, a couple of weeks after my seventeenth birthday, as I lay shivering in bed with a low-grade comedown, I picked up the phone to a whole new galaxy of misery; somehow my sister's husband had managed to drive his car off the road, killing him instantly and transforming my sister into a widowed mother of two young children at the age of twenty-two. A few weeks later she moved back north to be closer to her family – finally acquiescing to the web of tragedy that had long since swaddled us all, its sticky silken strands stretching all the way back to that fateful summer's morning eight years earlier. The day our world had ended and begun.

Year Zero.

As for my poor, sweet, broken mother? Well she did

eventually come down from her room. At least her body did. Her mind on the other hand remained resolutely locked away upstairs somewhere, cold and distant. Out of reach. Gone were the fun-time breakfasts, the girly nights in painting our toenails and straightening each other's hair. Stolen. Instead my formerly glamorous mummy had been replaced by a lank-haired, dead-eyed zombie, shuffling listlessly around the house or to the supermarket and back, her mouth flecked with white spit from the head pills, taking slow, shallow gulps of air like an oxygen-starved goldfish, resigned to her fate, going round and round and round...

And completely ignoring me.

Oh yes, your poor mother was left to stagger along the pot-holed pavement of adolescence almost entirely un-aided and un-abetted. My first period, my first boyfriend, unexpected eruptions on my face and chest – all of these aberrations were met with little support bar the under-informed whispers of my classmates and the problem pages of Seventeen *magazine. Needless to say, I spent the majority of my teenage years feeling conflicted about exactly what I was and wasn't supposed to be doing, more often than not getting it spectacularly wrong.*

Not that I was alone in feeling like this. As I've said before, Year Zero left a sizeable hole in most families, and at least half of my friends had lost one if not both parents to the Monsters. Now in theory, this should have made things easier. There should have been a sense of solidarity amongst survivors, a whole network of people to hold out their arms and catch us as we fell: councillors, seminars, how-to-not-fuck-up-your-life manuals handed out at the school gates. And I suppose there might have been those things, if any of us had the energy or inclination to go and look for them. But ultimately I guess we were too damaged and self-obsessed to ask for help. Besides, it was bad enough having to share my personal tragedy with what felt like half the world without having my face rubbed in the ignominy of group grieving sessions. It was like Dad's death – and my subsequent delinquency – had been co-opted by newspaper columnists and national memorials. None of it belonged to me anymore. We were simply statistics to be wheeled out during debates on foreign policy; our ruined family a coloured slice on some politician's pie chart. Which is why, I suppose, I spent so many years feeling so unspeakably angry.

In fact, I was fucking furious.

At the politicians, the papers, at Dad for getting himself killed and at Mum for going crazy. I was angry with my school, with my sister, with the government and with my friends. But most of all, I was angry with the Monsters. Many a night I would lie awake, vividly picturing the things I'd do if I was left alone in a room with just one of them, so much so that even when I found sleep my dreams would be stained with green blood and severed tails. Oh, I'd make them suffer if I got the chance.

Except as far as I could tell, there were no Monsters around. At least not recently. Sure there were reports of their activities – road-side bombs, attacks on schools and hospitals – as well as the occasional well-publicised arrests of a few low-level collaborators, but when it came to nailing the big boys, they always seemed to drift away and vanish, like smoke pouring from the side of an overturned tank. Even the army couldn't seem to find them, the news reports filled with bored-looking soldiers and politicians defending their on-going occupation of yet another stretch of barren foreign soil, sweating into their expensive suits as they promised to leave no stone unturned, giving cryptic warnings of the horrors that lay in store if they were to walk away:

'We might be winning the war… but the war is still a long way from won.'

Every so often, news would leak of some new atrocity committed by our boys out in the desert; a secret torture facility or a group of locals that had been rounded up and shot. Generally though, everyone was in agreement. The ends justified the means. There were *Monsters out there – hiding in the hills, being sheltered in caves maybe – it was just a case of finding them. And bringing them to justice. Until then there was nothing left to do except*

Wait.

And wait we did, the months and years tumbling by in a blur of beer and bourbon, the hangovers and resentment growing in stature until finally I found myself twenty-one years old, peering into the precipice of my final exams. But was I at home studying? Diligently making notes and revising? Of course I wasn't. No, as if sensing the end of an era, and the looming of a new and even more terrifying phase – of adulthood and responsibility – I was out drinking, burying my head in a bucket of booze, desperately trying to hang on to the last, splintering fragments of my youth. Refusing to grow up, whatever the cost. Which is how I found myself sprawled out at some downtown house party at 3am, surrounded by a bunch of guys I'd never seen before in my life.

To call it a house was probably pushing it. It certainly wasn't a home. Most of the windows had been smashed and repaired with taped-up plastic bags, staining what little light spilled in from the streetlamps outside a strange artificial blue. Looking out, it felt like you were inside a giant bubble, a self-contained pod operating outside boring grown-up conventions like night and day, or summer or winter. The only time here was 'party time', the sole condition of entry: extreme and debilitating intoxication.

This free-flowing philosophy extended to the interior of the house, the rooms refusing to be defined by societal expectations. There wasn't a kitchen or lounge per se; rather rooms seemed to run into each other, with great chunks of plaster missing from the partition walls creating a sort of open-plan network of spaces where people lay sprawled on the floor, or danced on the stairs, or vomited against walls, or fucked in darkened corners. On the back of the front door someone had graffitied an enormous lime green penis. It was difficult to imagine people actually living here.

As I stared blearily at the chaos unfolding all around me, I happened upon a small pocket of clarity. I realised I had no idea how I'd got here. I tried to retrace the evening's events but it was no good; the holes in my memory were bigger than those in the crumbling wall I was propped against. The girl I'd gone out with eight or nine hours earlier was nowhere to be seen and the people I was standing with now appeared to be speaking German. Wie geht es dir? *one of them asked, clamping an arm around my shoulder to stop me toppling over. I shrugged him off, fumbling for the bottle he was holding out and taking a long hit, a flavourless paint-thinner burn bringing tears to my eyes. I handed it back and staggered off to look for a bathroom, or somewhere to lie down. Picking my way across the filthy floor, being careful to take a wide arc around the people dancing in the centre of the room, I approached one of the larger wall-holes and hoisted myself through, disappearing into the darkness.*

I blinked once, twice, my eyes struggling to adjust to the light, which was even dimmer than on the other side of the wall. Rather than a bathroom, I appeared to have stumbled on some sort of makeshift chill-out room, a circle of bodies lying stretched out on a ragged assortment of beanbags and old mattresses. It was quieter in here, the harsh dance music blaring in the other room now reduced to a muffled, guttural thump. Squinting to see if I recognised any of the people on the floor, I was distracted by a faint blue flickering in the centre of the circle. Intrigued, I took a step forward and stooped down, my senses immediately assaulted by a dank, musky odour. 'Hey,' somebody said, handing me a bottle as I perched on the edge of the mattress. I took a quick hit, then another, my head starting to buzz nicely again as I tried to make sense of the unfamiliar ritual unfolding in front of me.

The guy was my age, a couple of years older maybe, though he'd probably have passed for mid-forties; the tell-

tale black circles around his eyes and mottled grey complexion reminding me of a corpse I'd seen on some detective show once, a badly made-up extra laid out on the slab. I wondered how long he'd been at the party. I watched as his fingers worked quickly to fold a sheet of aluminium foil in two before he produced a lighter, delicately stroking the silver creases with the flame, being careful not to linger in any one spot for too long. Once he was satisfied, he reached down and produced a small wrap of clingfilm, expertly shaking a line of off-white powder into the shallow ridge he'd created. I felt a spasm of excitement in my chest. This was something I'd only ever seen before in movies, or caught whispers about in the playground. It was a dark, wicked thing; forbidden, fantastic – the slippery slope your parents warned you about.

I took another hit from the bottle.

The man was holding something in his mouth now, a wrinkled, stubby tube that also looked like it had been fashioned from foil, and as I leaned closer he again lifted the lighter and sparked it to life, the blue flame illuminating the stiff expression on his face. There was no anticipation there, no longing. Only a grim determination, like a carpenter eyeing a loose floorboard that needed fixing.

Then raising the hammer to strike the nail.

He brought the lighter closer to the foil and then, in one startlingly quick movement, he bent forward and traced under the line of powder with the flame, jerking his head in order to catch every last curl of smoke that rose up from the bubbling mess where the powder had been, his face finally alive, lips curling in blissed-out satisfaction as he clutched at his straining chest, dampening a cough before finally exhaling a thin shadow in my direction.

And then he looked up.

'You want some?' he asked, like we were splitting a sandwich, or a chocolate bar. I didn't answer, a ripple of movement in the shadows suggesting there were others waiting impatiently for an offer. But the man didn't seem to

notice, his fingers already moving automatically, refolding foil, emptying powder, the whole procedure conducted with an almost medical detachment so that it was hard to get excited or to feel worried about any of it until suddenly the man was holding out the foil tube for me to take and saying, 'Just make sure you suck it all up. Don't let any get away.' And I just sat there, frozen, drunk, tired, scared, angry.

Twenty-one.

And so I shrugged and said, 'Fuck it,' and took his stupid tube. And held it to my lips. And closed my eyes. And listened for the sound of the spark. And then:

'Wait!'

I opened my eyes, managing to spill the powder from the foil as I turned towards the sound of the voice. The dead-faced man swore loudly, scrambling to his knees in a desperate attempt to save some of the dust from falling between the floorboards. But I didn't care. Because I was staring at the man who had just walked into the room – well, a boy really – tall, clean-cut, wearing a shirt and tie of all things. He was like a dream, a vision. He was the most beautiful boy I'd ever seen. And he was talking to me. He said:

'You want to get out of here.'

It wasn't a question.

* * *

There were three choices, like a fuckin game show or somethin – pick A, B or C to win a prize. Only there was no luxury Caribbean holiday waitin in a golden envelope for us if we picked the right one. Jus' the chance to swat away the vultures that had been circlin overhead ever since the attack.

Choice A was the simplest. We stayed put and did nothin. Now on first inspection, this wasn't as dumb an idea as it sounded. After all, we were due to arrive at the airfield the next night. When we didn't show up a search team would immediately be deployed to recover us and – ta-dah! – we'd be back home in time for breakfast the next day.

Sounds like a no-brainer, huh? Except this all relied on some bright spark actually noticin our absence amongst an influx of 100,000 personnel and then havin the fuckin brains to realise that our not being there actually signified a problem. Even then, should we be lucky enough to have Billy Brainbox put two and two together and send out a team to look for us, who knows if they'd actually be able to find us? Once we laid out our equipment in the light, we found that Jim was right – nearly all of it had either been destroyed or stolen.

What's more, the bastards seemed to have specifically targeted our tech equipment: GPS, satellite phone, radio – basically anything we could use to contact the outside world was gone, as was anything that could be used to track us. Our rations too had been hit, as had our water supplies. And of course the tents were all shot up as well, meaning we didn't have any shelter. Pretty much the only things that remained intact were our weapons, which looked like they hadn't been touched at all. In fact, we now had far more guns and ammunition than we could carry, owin to everyone bein dead and all. At least if things got too desperate out here there'd be no shortage of choice should we decide to finish ourselves off ha.

On the other hand we had options B and C – both of which involved a shitload of walkin. Option B, the one Jim favoured, meant walkin back to the base, retracin our steps as best we could and hopin to fuck we didn't get lost. Now this sounded like horseshit to me. Firstly we'd already walked two days to get out here, and we supposedly only had one day left before we hit the airstrip. This would mean walking an extra day if we followed Jim's plan, which considerin the food and water situation didn't sound like it made a fuck of a lot of sense. Secondly, what do ya think'd happen to us after we rocked up at the base in two days' time? Even if they believed our story and didn't lock us up for desertin or something, the best we could hope for was to be patched up and sent to join another platoon to ship out with. We'd be makin the journey twice for nothin!

All of which is why *my* choice – to carry on towards the airstrip – makes the most sense. Even taking it slowly, we should be able to reach it by the end of the day, or at the latest by tomorrow morning. Twelve hours. Which, considerin the state of our supplies, is about how long we're gonna last.

Despite all this though, Jim was adamant. He wanted us to turn around and walk back to base. God knows why. Probably wants to win himself a medal or somethin. *Sergeant Needle-Dick Saves the Day!* You see with the Lieutenant dead, Jim was technically the highest ranked among us. I didn't give a shit though. There was no way in hell I was gonna let some jumped up secretary pull rank and make me march an extra two days in the wrong direction. And so this mornin when he suggested we get goin, your daddy decided to use a bit of the ol' charm to explain my position to him.

'Fuck you Jim you fuckin cunt, we ain't fuckin goin. And don't even think about pullin rank on me, you shrivelled ol' fuck-stain of a fuck-up. You might be Sergeant of this platoon, but as far as I can tell, there ain't no fuckin platoon left. There's just five blokes sat in the desert,' I paused to jab a finger at Cal, Doggie and Jett, who were sat up on the bank, watchin with open mouths. 'And we ain't gonna starve to death jus' so you can win a medal. Now, we had orders to go to the airstrip. We're goin to the airstrip. You fuckin got it?'

We put it to a vote in the end, me and Jim with a line drawn in the sand between us. Neither of us said a thing as we stood there facin the boys. We didn't need to. Everyone knew the game. It was time to pick sides. Jett was first to move. Apparently he's only a year older than Cal, but you'd never believe it. He's a big lad is Jett, not just tall but stacked, athletic lookin. Whereas most of us are sunburnt, Jett is sun*kissed*, with these big blue eyes below a perfect handful of blond hair, jus' bout as long as regulations allow. Reckons he's a big-shot surfer back home, which wouldn't surprise me. He's got that look about him – sort of a fake southern stoner charm thing goin on. Course he's a real hit with the ladies. The fellas too I wouldn't wonder, what with that hair. Yep, you'd have to try real hard to hate ol' Jett. But I just about manage it, ha.

'Okay then folks,' Jett said, hoppin to his feet and flashin a set of perfectly white teeth. 'So I hate to be a dick, Corporal, but I think the Staff Sergeant has a point. And seein as he's the highest ranked officer and all…' He trailed off as he sauntered over to Jim's side of the line. And then, once he was stood next to him, the fucker winked at me. I ain't kiddin – he actually winked at me! Well I just gave him a great big grin and shrugged my shoulder, silently wishing bowel cancer on him and his entire fuckin family.

Next up was Cal. The poor kid'd managed to get some clothes on by now, but he still looked shell-shocked, his rabbit-wild eyes glued to the dirt as he got up and shuffled over to me. 'I jus' wanna go home,' he mumbled as I gave him a gentle dig in the arm.

That just left Doggie.

Now I've known Doggie for about five years for my sins. See, I'm not convinced there's much goin on behind that big, dumb face of his. Doggie likes motorbikes. Doggie likes animals. Doggie likes his beer cold, his meals hot and his women *smokin', baby!* And that's about it. If you were feeling generous you might say he's a man of simple pleasures. On the other hand you might just call him a fat retard. What's more, he insists on presentin himself as one of those sickeningly cheerful fat guys, the kind who hides behind a shield of bad puns and wisecracks to deflect from the fact his cardiovascular system is groaning under the strain of keepin his fat ass vertical. I looked down at him, a little roll of belly hangin out over his belt. Fuck knows how he made Corporal. I guess they didn't know what else to do with him.

'Hmmm…' he said, scratchin at the thick stubble that speckled his several chins. 'Now let me get this straight.

Our GPS is smashed, our phones and radio gone. And we ain't got no map or compass neither?' This was true. In its eternal wisdom, the army no longer saw fit to equip us with basic tools like a map – not when there was a hi-tech version that allowed us to do all sorts of fancy tricks. Seems nobody had considered the eventuality that a group of bloodthirsty Monsters might reduce our kit to a pile of crushed microchips.

'And our food and water situation's lookin less than appealin,' Doggie continued. 'In fact I guess you could say we're up stink creek without a life jacket, uh-huh… ' I grimaced. 'Guess that's about the size of it, D… ' Doggie nodded to himself, pleased to have spelled out the fuckin obvious for nobody's benefit. 'Uh-huh,' he said again as he heaved himself up to his feet, lookin from me to Jim and back again like he hadn't already made up his mind, like he didn't know exactly where he was goin to place his cross. Right then I felt like steppin forward and slittin the fat cunt's throat, just to watch the look on his face.

'Well then… ' he says, takin a step towards us. 'I guess that only leaves one logical course of action… ' HURRY THE FUCK UP YOU FAT MOTHERFUCKIN PIECE OF SHIT. '… And in a way I'm sorry it has to come down to this…' I'm reachin for my gun now. I'm reachin for my gun and I'm gonna shoot him in the fuckin eye. '… Buuuuut… I'm gonna have to go with Corporal Parker on this one. The less time we're out here the better as far as I'm concerned. I'm sorry Jim… '

Good ol' Doggie. I knew he had it in him. He might be slow, but he's alright. 'Well then Sergeant,' I said as Doggie took his place next to me and Cal. 'It looks like democracy has spoken.' For a second I thought he was about to try and pull that highest rank shit again, but he just shrugged his shoulders and spat on the ground. 'Looks that way,' he said. 'Fuckin right it looks that way,' I snapped back. Sergeant or not, I ain't takin his shit. Then I turned to the rest of them. 'Looks like we're goin home boys!' Doggie of course started up then, letting out a loud 'Hell yeah!' while Cal and Jett just sort of mumbled and nodded.

Not that I blame 'em. To tell the truth son, it don't feel like much to celebrate. Not when there's so much blood in the sand. But we are comin home son. That's the main thing. And it won't be long now. It won't be long.

* * *

When somebody saves your life, the least you can do is buy them a drink. That was something your father used to say. And so that is how, as night edged towards day and the first commuters started heaving their way across town on a brisk, late-summer's morning, I found myself sat in a grimy twenty-four hour diner, cradling a lukewarm black coffee in my lap and spilling my guts to a smartly dressed stranger.

Little did I know then I was talking to your future daddy.

His name was Daniel – 'like the kid with the lions' – but he preferred Danny for short. Danny Parker. I asked him if he was religious and he said he wasn't sure. He believed in hell but didn't know about heaven. I asked if he thought that might make him a pessimist. He shrugged and laughed. 'Fucked if I know.' Mostly though, he was happy to let me do the talking. Which is just as well really, as with the booze still pumping through my system I was on a roll, hopping from subject to subject with total disregard for traditional narrative structure, taking in drinking, university, school, my dead dad and my clinically sad mother and sister, my hobbies and interests. 'Let me guess, heroin?' Danny said, flashing a rare, crooked smile. 'A drunken mistake that never happened,' I countered. 'Thanks to you.'

Our eyes met across the greasy counter.

Thanks to him.

Later on I asked your father why he called out to me in that scummy room, why out of all the girls who must have been at the party, he decided to try and save me. 'Because you looked like you wanted to be saved,' he answered, shooting me a look I'd get used to seeing – a look that meant I couldn't tell if he was joking or not. 'Plus I guessed you'd be an easy lay, ha.'

That morning, as the traffic rattled outside the diner window, growing progressively louder as the morning crawled on, neither of us felt the need to explain ourselves. He'd asked and I'd answered. That was all either of us needed to know. We spent another hour or so drinking industrial strength coffee, me talking and Danny listening, before the first shoots of a poisonous hangover broke the surface and threatened to strangle my monologue. I excused myself and made my way to the bathroom to splash my face with water.

When I returned to the table I saw that Danny had gathered his things together. 'Where are you going?' I asked, struggling to keep the panic out of my voice, unexpectedly frightened by the prospect of him leaving. Of being alone again. He stood up, pointing to his tie. 'Interview,' he explained. 'I can't be late. Plus, you look like you could do with a little sleep. No offence.' I felt my airway begin to constrict as I fumbled for the right words to make him stay, aware I was probably coming on a little psychotic. 'Bu-but,' I stammered, playing for time, desperately trying to keep the conversation going for another precious few seconds. 'What's the interview for?' Danny paused, seeming genuinely surprised by my interest. 'Oh. Well. I signed up a few months ago and I finally got the call a week or so ago. I've already passed my medical. It's my selection interview today. I'm going to be... '

A soldier.

'That's great,' I gushed, uncertain if it was but desperate to keep him talking all the same. 'Are you nervous?' But it was no good, Danny was already backing away from me. 'Look I'm sorry Lorna, I've really got to go.' Swallowing down my embarrassment I stood up, deciding to go for broke. 'But don't you want to... meet up again?' To my horror he gave a little laugh – ha – and turned away. 'Wait!' I called, far too loud, people around us looking up from their breakfasts.

But Danny kept walking.

I felt the breath crushed from my lungs. I glanced down. And lying right in front of me, amongst the squeezy condiment bottles and sticky coffee rings, was a crumpled, white napkin, on it a phone number scrawled in scratchy, child-like handwriting. 'Call me, okay?' Danny called as he reached the door. I fell back into my chair, carefully folding the napkin safely away. 'Okay,' I said, finally allowing myself a small, relieved smile, before I suddenly remembered something.

'Good luck!' I yelled after him.

But he was already gone

Over the next few weeks I met up with Danny almost every night, sometimes to drink coffee and sometimes to drink beer and sometimes just to sit in the passenger seat of his car while he drove in long, looping circles around the city, going nowhere in particular, pushing his old, beat-up coupé to the point where the engine started to scream and my teeth rattled in their gums. But wherever we were, it was always the same; I'd talk and Danny would listen. Every so often I'd try and get him to open up, to tell me about his family – about anything – but he would just shrug and mumble or change the subject. Which if I'm honest suited me just fine. I had plenty of conversation for the both of us. And hey – he was cheaper than a therapist. Anyway, he seemed happy enough with the arrangement and, without making any conscious decisions or even really discussing it out loud, we started going steady.

In many ways Danny was the ideal boyfriend; he was clean, polite and kind. The sex – while not earth-shaking – was good. He was a considerate, efficient lover, though I sometimes got the sense he was holding something back from me. There seemed to be a distance between us, no matter how close our physical proximity. Still, I always came. He wasn't pushy either, which made a nice difference from the overexcited, puppy-like boys I'd known at university. In fact if anything it always seemed to be me chasing after him, trying to pin him down. But maybe that was just the way he liked it.

It was hard to tell with Danny.

Once my exams were out the way (it's fair to say they went badly, although not quite *as badly as they might have), I decided to stay with Danny rather than moving back in with Mum, and as the months rolled by we found ourselves falling into a comfortable routine. We found a small apartment and I took a job at a local call centre to pay my share of the rent, Danny preferring instead to eat into his savings, spending his days working out in the gym. After my shifts he would pick me up and we'd go and watch a movie or have a drink before returning home.*

And even though my job was soul-destroyingly dull, and the war on the TV blazed ever more brutally, the journalists now teaching the nation an entirely new vocabulary – one filled with 'friendly fire' and 'covert death squads' – life was nevertheless pretty peachy for those few months. I even dared to start dreaming of a little long-term happiness, just like the song:

Danny and Lorna sitting in a tree
K-I-S-S-I-N-G
First came love, then came marriage
Then came…

Then came a fucking great bombshell that ripped through the centre of everything, leaving my happy-ever-after a tattered, bloody mess.

I had been in work for less than an hour, but already the morning shift was dragging painfully. I'd recently been transferred to outbound sales – cold calling through a list of random numbers and desperately trying to convince the hapless recipient of why they needed *a certain financial product in their life – and I was finding it particularly tough. It wasn't that I blamed people for being rude. It was just I found I could only take being invited to insert a low-interest credit card or tax-free savings scheme into my most intimate enclaves so many times a day before I became a little jaded. Anyway, for whatever reason that morning's customers seemed particularly cantankerous and, as I sat there passively absorbing the howls of abuse, I allowed myself to indulge in my favourite office fantasy, that of tearing the headset from my ear and instigating a workers' uprising, kicking over every filing cabinet and artificial pot plant as we marched on our way to freedom – or at least to the pub – when suddenly I looked up to find my line manager standing next to my desk.*

Looking very uncomfortable indeed.

'Would you mind coming with me?' he asked as I finished the call, steering me towards one of the small, suffocating interview rooms in the corner of the office. He turned on the light and told me to take a seat as he drew the blinds, even asking me if I'd like a glass of water.

And then he told me my sister had called.

Three hours later I was on a train back home. Mum had suffered a sudden and severe myocardial infarction – a heart attack – and was lying unconscious in intensive care. My sister was already by her side but her chances didn't look good. Apparently she'd been unconscious for at least an hour before she was discovered.

Guilt.

Thick and sickly, it coated my tongue and trickled down my neck as I waited for a taxi to take me from the station to the hospital. My mummy was going to die and it was all my fault. Perhaps if I'd been a good daughter, if I'd stayed at home and looked after her she'd have clung on for another few years. But instead I'd run away to get drunk and high and chase after boys. I hated myself. But even more than that, I hated the Monsters – those sick green bastards who'd done this to her, who'd taken Daddy away and ruined our lives and broken her heart.

I got there as fast as I could.

But like always, I arrived a couple of minutes too late.

I stayed at home with my sister and the girls for the next few weeks. For a city well versed in tragedy, there was still an extraordinary amount of legal hoopla for us to negotiate; a task made all the more difficult by the origami of paperwork Mum had left behind. Eventually though we managed to untangle it all, and once the funeral was over and every last dotted line was signed and countersigned, I allowed myself a couple of days of lying on the sofa, crying in a crumpled heap.

And then I got back on a train.

I was vaguely worried about seeing Danny again after everything that had happened. I hadn't even told him I was leaving – I'd gone straight to the station from work in the clothes I was wearing – and with all the drama I'd barely had a chance to speak to him beyond a couple of vague, monosyllabic telephone calls. Now I was back, I was scared he might have moved on, perhaps even having found someone else; someone light and breezy. Someone fun. *Someone who crucially didn't have the stigma of a dead Mum to add to their ever expanding list of woes.*

Danny greeted me as I walked into the apartment and at first it seemed that my fears were well-founded. He looked serious, his face twisted into a brooding expression I'd never seen before. In his hand was a letter, and for a second I had a horrible vision of him handing me my notice:

Sorry Lorna, I'm restructuring.

Downsizing.

Optimising.

There's really no easy way to say this:

You're out.

But then the storm lifted and he smiled and held up the envelope so I could see the official stamp on the front. 'I got it!' he said. 'I passed! Can you believe it? I start basic training two weeks from now – I'm going to be a soldier!' I rushed to hug him, the relief that I was not being dumped drowning out all of my concerns about the practicalities of his new job – like the fact it would mean yet more time apart. Like the fact he could get killed. Or kill someone. Instead I told him how great he was, how he deserved it after all of the hard work he'd put in, how it was fucking excellent news. *'There's something else,' he said, peeling me off him and holding me lightly by the wrists, his face suddenly serious again. My heart stopped. I'd been wrong about everything:*

He didn't think it was working.

It wasn't me, it was him.

He took a deep breath.

'I think we should get married.'

* * *

We started off a little before midday, packing anythin we thought might be useful for the journey. Food, water and weapons mainly. Plus my notebook of course. The rest of it we left behind, neither havin the energy nor the stomach to wash the blood off of everythin else. Anyhow, there didn't seem much point in weighin ourselves down for such a short journey. There was some debate about what to do with the bodies, whether we should bury 'em or burn 'em, but in the end we decided it would take too long and so we just draped them in what was left of the tents, securin the ragged canvas with rocks. We figured the army would be out here soon enough to collect 'em and ship 'em off to the families. Jim insisted we mumble a few words before we left, commending their poor souls to the mercy of God and what not, and then we were gone, spreadin out in a loose line as we settled into our own pace, me at the front and Doggie at the back, all of us thinkin: here we go again.

Now you might think there ain't much to look at in the desert, like when you get to the end of the story and all you've got left to flick through are those blank pages they stick in to make the book look bigger. But you'd be wrong. There's plenty to see in the desert. In fact, I could probably fill a whole fuckin library describin all the things I've seen, from anthills higher than my head to the bloom of desert roses. I ain't kiddin – simple things like the shifting patterns of the clouds or the different textures of rocks can be enough to keep you entertained for hours. Well, actually I don't know if it'd keep you entertained. There's not a screen or a flashin light in sight, ha. But it's enough for me. And even when you get tired of lookin at everythin that's out here, the desert's a great place to spend time lookin at all the things that *ain't* there.

What I mean is you can use all that endless sand and sky as a canvas and paint a picture. A bit like you do with your crayons, only you gotta use your mind instead. For instance, if I want to see a steak dinner I just stare out and relax my eyes and BOOM! What d'ya know? I got me a nice juicy T-bone, pink in the middle jus' the way I like it. Same if I wanna watch a ball game, or visit a girly bar, or anythin else ya can think of. I could even paint a picture of your mother if I wanted to. If I felt like makin myself sick that is ha. I used to do somethin similar when I was a kid, starin at the static between TV stations. I'd make up my own cartoons, better than any of the crappy shows that used to be on. I'd sit for hours and do it.

Anyway, it's the same here. Only thing I can't seem to picture properly is you for some reason. It always clouds over and gets fuzzy whenever I try. I guess maybe 'cos you're always growin and stuff, changin. Maybe you could paint a picture of yourself for me and send it. Maybe that would help.

As the day slowly wore on, midday becomin afternoon becomin evenin, it became clear we weren't gonna make the strip before nightfall. None of us said anythin though. Nah. We just kept on marchin until it was pitch black and our feet hurt and our teeth were chatterin from it bein so freezin fuckin cold. Even then we just kept on goin. In the end it was Cal of all people who put into words what everyone was thinkin. 'We're fuckin lost.' It wasn't a question, and nobody argued. Instead we just stopped walkin and bunched together, everyone eyeballin me all of a sudden like they expected me to tell 'em what we should do next. I looked at Doggie and

Cal, their teeth chatterin, their eyes wide with expectation. Christ, even Jett looked like he was open to suggestions. Finally I looked over at Jim and shrugged. 'Why don't you ask the Staff Sergeant if he's got any bright ideas?'

In the end we figured it would be safer to bunk down for the night and wait until the mornin. Course we didn't have any tents with us, and it was too late to start a fire, so we did the best we could. We dug a shallow trench to protect us from the wind and sat back to back, tryin to preserve our body heat. Some bed, huh? To tell the truth, it felt more like we was climbing into our own grave. Needless to say I didn't sleep.

We were up and walkin again before daybreak. Like I said, we'd finished the last of our rations the night before so breakfast consisted of a mouthful of warm water. We didn't even have a fuckin toothbrush between us. Still, I was glad to be up and out of that pit. Doggie in particular had started to stink like a rancid ham and I wanted to put as much distance between him and me as possible. I was glad there was only another couple of hours left to go, and made up my mind that once we landed I'd never see any of these fuckers again. Even if they tried to give us a medal, I wouldn't show up to the ceremony. I'd get 'em to post it. Anyway I'm guessin everyone was thinkin the same thing as for the rest of the day we walked in silence, one leg in font of the other, the landscape as empty as our bellies.

You know, back in basic trainin we spent a full week learnin about foragin. A week! Shit, I could tell ya how to distinguish between edible and poisonous berries if ya happened to find yourself lost in a low-lying deciduous forest, or how to prepare a broth from seaweed with enough nutrients to keep a man alive for a coupla months. I can tell a rabbit's tracks from a weasel's, and show you how to catch and skin either. Or how to make a coarse flour by pounding acorns with a rock, or how to dig an evaporation trap to purify water if you don't happen to have any iodine tablets handy.

But what I was never shown how to do, what nobody ever thought to teach me, is how the fuck I'm supposed to survive when all there is around me is sand. I mean it, that's literally *all* there is in this part of the country. No cactus to tap for water, no shrubs to harvest – shit it ain't rained here in about a half a century. The best I could do was pick up a smooth flat pebble and jam it under my tongue. It's an old sand-nigger trick I think. Supposed to stimulate your salivary glands or somethin. At the very least I guess it forces ya to breathe through your nose so you don't dry out as quick. Now there's a tip for ya son, should ya ever find ever yourself wanderin through the desert starvin and thirsty. Stick a rock in your mouth. You can pass that advice on to your mother too if you like. Might shut her up for once ha.

Well you've probably guessed by now that the airstrip turned out to be more than two hours away and by early evenin we were still walkin, our hopes of ever makin it there fadin quicker than the light. As usual I was at the front of the pack, not thinkin 'bout much in particular, when out of nowhere I sensed movement to the left of me. Instictively I reached for my rifle, just in time to see Cal sprintin wildly past me, his limbs skitterin and scatterin all over the place like he's havin some sort of a seizure.

Naturally I presumed he'd lost the plot again, when I heard a sound behind me and turned to see Jett was runnin too, followed by Jim. Even Doggie had caught up from the back, coughin his lungs up as he pumped his arms and legs for all he was worth. I shot out an arm as he reached me, grabbin him roughly by the shoulder 'Hey, what the fuck?' I asked, glancing nervously behind him. I half expected to see a swarm of Monsters chasin after us, but when I looked back at Dog he was grinnin idiotically at me. I tightened my grip on him, pinchin a fat fold of flesh between my nails as I waited for an answer. He yowled as he shrugged me off, pointing in the direction Cal, Jett and Jim had disappeared. 'Look...'

I squinted, following his podgy finger until finally I saw it. I shook my head, amazed I hadn't spotted it earlier, but before I could say anythin Doggie was gone, wobblin after the others and leavin me starin open mouthed after him. Because risin up in the distance, not more than a coupla kilometers away, was the unmistakable outline of clay huts, a dozen or so simple stone chimneys juttin out against the charcoal sky. It was a village.

Now if this was a made-up story son, I would probably think about knockin it on the head right around here. Yup, I'd write you a nice warm fuzzy endin describin how we stumbled across a tribe of simple, peace lovin people who showered us with food and shelter before providin us with our exact coordinates and a secure phone line to contact our superior officers back at base. And then I'd sit back and collect my royalty cheque once Disney had decided to turn it into an animated movie, complete with a litter of talkin piglets who laughed and told jokes as they basted themselves in BBQ sauce and then hopped onto a spit.

But of course this ain't a story, and a quick tour of the village told me everythin I needed to know. It was a small settlement, maybe thirty separate buildins arranged in a spiral around what was presumably once a bustlin central square. Now though, the place was little more than a dusty pit, with large cracks runnin through the earth and a rash of ancient bullet holes pepperin the face of the crumblin houses. The place looked like it had been abandoned years ago – maybe even before the war. Either way, it didn't look like there'd be any pigs around there, talkin or otherwise.

'Hey – there's nobody here!'

I turned to see Doggie pokin his head out of a doorway, a look on his face like he'd just invented the atom bomb. 'Really?' I said, resistin the urge to go over there and tear out his windpipe. 'Nah,' he said, bumblin on obliviously. 'Looks like everybody cleared out a while ago. I did find this little fella though.' Doggie stooped down for a moment and then reappeared, a small bundle of rags clutched tightly to his chest. I stepped forward, squinting until finally I saw a scrawny, scared-lookin kitten, no bigger than a rat. 'She was out the back here. I thought she was dead at first, poor thing. I'm gonna call her Lucky.' 'Very original,' I shrugged. 'Uh-huh. I think she's hungry,' Doggie said, pettin her clumsily with his enormous hands. 'We're all fuckin hungry,' I snapped. 'Tell her to join the back of the queue.'

Jus' then Jett came struttin out into the main square flanked by Cal. 'Hey there Dog,' he called out. 'I didn't think you liked pussy… ' I have to admit it was pretty funny – at least for Jett – and we all laughed while Doggie stood there sulkin, cooin sweet nothins into the ear of his fuckin cat. 'Ah relax,' Jett said, once he'd got his breath back. 'I'm jus' fuckin with you. If anythin I'd say your new friend is a piece of luck. I mean, there must be water nearby for it to survive out here, wouldn't ya say? Not that we found any. There's a well round the back but it's drier than Doggie's mum's fur burger.' We all laughed again. 'Okay, fuckin knock it off!' Doggie growled, takin a step towards Jett. 'Or what?' Jett answered, 'You gonna make me?' I tried to decide who I thought would win out of the two of them in a brawl. Even though Jett was obviously taller and fitter, Doggie had more weight behind him. Looked like he'd throw one hell of a punch. Either way, it'd be somethin to watch.

A loud yell from the other side of the square interrupted them. 'THAT'S ENOUGH LADIES…' We all turned to see Jim makin his way towards us. 'We've got more than enough problems without you two actin like a pair of bitches. It looks like the camel-fuckers abandoned this festering shit heap at least a hundred years ago. We're out of food and we're almost out of water. Now I reckon we bed down in one of these huts for the night and in the morning we… holy shit Corporal, is that a cat you're holding? I didn't think you liked pussy?'

You gotta hand it to Jim – his timing was perfect. I thought Cal was gonna have a fuckin seizure he was laughin so hard.

Suddenly there was a sharp squawk, followed by a flash of fur as the kitten shot across the square and disappeared into one of the houses. 'You fuckin pricks!' Doggie yelled, holdin up his hand to show a long scratch down the side of his arm, a thin trickle of blood runnin down towards his elbow. 'You fuckin scared her… '

We fell silent for a moment as we watched Doggie lumber off after his precious cat, desperately callin her as he ran. 'Here Lucky… C'mon Lucky.' As he passed I got a look at his face, his eyes all red as if he were about to start blubberin any minute. We watched him disappear then looked away, kickin the dirt, not sayin anythin.

* * *

It was a small wedding. Danny had explained how he didn't want too much of a fuss, which suited me just fine seeing as I only had my sister and nieces left to invite. Danny was an only child and his mum had passed when he was young, so there wasn't much of an issue on his side either. The only odd one was his dad. I'd only ever heard him talk about him once, late one night when he'd come back wasted – something he'd been doing more and more often since being called up. He'd told me this story about how when he was a kid his 'old man' used to get so drunk and violent that Danny took to sleeping in his tree house. Apparently one night he woke to a loud crack and looked down to see his dad stood at the bottom of the tree, axe in hand. Danny just about managed to scramble free from the branches before the whole thing came crashing down, wiping out half their garage in the process.

It sounded horrific, but the whole time he was talking Danny laughed his head off, like it was the funniest thing in the world. However, any time I'd tried to bring up the topic of his father since, he'd tensed up and changed the subject. I didn't even know whether he was alive or dead, and so when the wedding came round and Danny didn't mention him I decided it was best to follow suit.

In the end it was just the seven of us who stood huddled in the small, grey council offices one wet September morning; Me, Danny, my sister, my nieces and the judge, plus an old drinking buddy of Danny's called Mike, who we drafted in at the last minute when we realised we were a witness short. The whole ceremony was over in twenty minutes and we held our reception – which Mike hilariously insisted on calling 'the wake' – at a bar around the corner. From there we headed straight off on our honeymoon, which in reality consisted of two nights at a budget motel about three blocks from our apartment. Still, the whole thing was a lot of fun. We took some good photos and I got to pretend I was a grown-up for a few days. Plus Danny was unbelievably sweet, most of the time. Only on one occasion did things threaten to turn ugly, when the receptionist at the motel, a sweet, brown skinned girl, mixed up our dinner reservation. Danny started muttering under his breath, a deluge of dark, disgusting words I'd never heard him use before oozing out of his mouth before he caught the look on my face and shrugged it off as a joke.

Mostly though things were great, with Danny making all these grand statements about how we were a 'real family now' and how he'd always 'honour and protect me' and all this other clichéd nonsense I'm sure he'd only ever heard people say to each other in movies. Honestly, he gave me a run for my money in the melodrama stakes.

But the saddest thing of all?

I believed him.

Once our honeymoon was over we went back to the apartment and Danny set about packing up his things. He only had a couple of days before he was due to begin training and regardless of what he said I could tell he was nervous, folding and refolding his clothes dozens of times until they took up the smallest possible space in his trunk. He was touchy too. One evening we were sat together when a current affairs programme came on the TV, two middle-aged white men yelling at each other in front of a live studio audience. I reached for the remote control, knocking up the volume as I tried to follow the thread of their argument. One of the men was stood up behind his desk, jabbing his finger at the other man as he demanded for all troops to return home with immediate effect. Before he could finish though, the screen went blank. I turned to find Danny gripping the remote so tightly his hand was shaking, the veins bulging in his powerful neck. 'What the hell?' I said. 'I was watching that.' Danny didn't answer though, jumping up and disappearing to the bedroom without a word. It was only once he'd gone that I realised he'd taken the remote with him.

The next morning I woke early to find I was alone in bed. Now this wasn't entirely unheard of – I knew Danny had trouble sleeping sometimes – yet for some reason I had a bad feeling. My mouth dry, I crept out of the bedroom to investigate, terrified I was about to find Danny hurt, or still angry from the night before. Or worse:

Gone.

As I tip-toed into the kitchen I was relieved to see him sat there, looking happy. To my surprise, the table had also been laid for breakfast, a decadent feast fanned out across the crisp white table cloth: freshly squeezed orange juice, croissants, toast, a range of condiments heaped in small silver pots I didn't even know we owned. 'I couldn't sleep,' Danny said by way of explanation. 'Maybe you shouldn't sleep more often!' I said, taking a seat and helping myself to a slice of toast. 'This is incredible!' It was then I noticed the brush resting in Danny's hand.

'I didn't know you were an artist?' I leant round him to get a better view of the small, wet-looking painting lying next to his empty plate. 'It's nothing,' he shrugged, dipping his brush into a glass, a blue mist unravelling in the water. 'When I was a kid I used to paint sometimes. In the tree house. I just felt like trying again... '

I scrunched up my face, trying to make sense of the smudge of primary colours. 'What is it?' I asked. He held up the picture for me to see. 'It's us,' he said, pointing to a pair of stick figures sat on a small blob of yellow. 'Or it will be. This is an island. You see the palm tree, the sandcastles? Once I'm finished with the army I reckon we should move. Look for the good life – sun, sand…' 'Sea?' I smiled, pointing to a scrappy patch of blue. 'Exactly,' he said. I stared at the painting. It was rough and child-like, but kind of sweet at the same time. I could tell he'd put some time into it. 'It's good,' I said. 'It's like a Picasso or something. I like it. But who's this?' Further on down the page was a smaller figure, one stick leg outstretched towards a blob of baby-blue sea. Danny grinned awkwardly. 'Ah,' he said. 'That's somebody who doesn't exist yet. That's… '

Our son.

The day Danny left I cried for eight hours straight. It was weird – the whole time he was packing, even when I drove him down to the bus station and kissed him goodbye and stood there waving with all the other heartbroken wives and girlfriends and mothers, I kept telling myself it was a good thing. *It was fourteen weeks out of a lifetime together. It was nothing. Most of all, it was what Danny wanted.*

It wasn't until I got back to the apartment that I fell apart. I think it was the sight of our bed that did it, the pillow still creased from where his head had lain only a few hours before. Instantly I felt all of my courage dissolve. I was bereaved all over again – lost and alone in the world. I pulled out one of Danny's dirty gym shirts from the wash and wrapped it around me, enveloping myself in his scent as the self-pity bubbled from my nose and eyes, sobbing in a small, pathetic heap on the bed until it got dark.

And then I got up and pulled myself together.

The first thing I did was quit my job. I'd hardly been in since I'd returned from my mum's funeral, but that wasn't going to deny me the satisfaction of walking into my manager's office and officially resigning. While it wasn't quite the socialist uprising I'd fantasised about (my manager shook my hand and promised me a good reference), I nevertheless took satisfaction in walking out of the building with my head held high, determined never to return. With my job out of the way, I was free to start planning my next move. Miraculously, Mum actually had some life insurance in place when she died, and even once her many creditors were paid off there was still a fairly substantial sum left over. In other words, I didn't need *to work, a situation which, while on one hand was unbelievably fortunate, also made me realise I had no idea what I wanted to do with my life.*

I passed the days trawling the internet and local papers, trying and failing to find something to capture my imagination and fill up my time (should I learn Mandarin? Study astrophysics? Develop my assertiveness?), while starting to wonder if this was perhaps why so many lottery winners ended up killing themselves. It wasn't as if I was suddenly, fabulously rich – I'd calculated that even pulling my belt in I'd only manage about eighteen months before I'd need to start looking for paid work again – yet without the daily drudge of a steady routine, with no mundane chores to occupy my mental processes, I could quite easily imagine myself going into a tailspin. Getting up that little bit later each morning, pouring my drinks that little bit stiffer. Now that I had all this time on my hands – and more importantly, this freedom to think – I found that I didn't actually have that much to think about. Which is why, in desperation more than anything, I found myself entering a dingy social club early one Monday morning, looking for the headquarters of the Military Spouses Meet-up Club.

The website had made it sound like a lot of fun. There would be wine tasting, karaoke, shopping trips, movie nights; all in the company of women who 'understood the privileges and responsibilities of having a partner serving in the armed forces'. I'd had an image of a warm circle of women –

sisters in solidarity – nights out and giggles and advice and sympathy. It would be like having a family again.

However, when I finally located the drab, nicotine-stained meeting room I found myself staring at six miserable faces; hollow husks of women, all of them at least two decades older than me. Realising I'd made a terrible mistake, I immediately tried to back away through the doors, but it was too late. One of them had noticed me and was gesturing for me to come inside. Swallowing down my misgivings, I forced a big fake smile on to my face and introduced myself to the group. 'Hi everybody, my name's Lorna... ' I said. One of the other women glanced up from her magazine and looked me over suspiciously. 'If you're lookin for AA sweetie, it's next door.'

The meeting that followed was undoubtedly the longest hour of my life. After the women had introduced themselves (or rather, introduced their husbands, all of them having the same weird habit of stating their partner's job title rather than their own name, as if they only existed as a sort of appendage to their husband's career) we played a couple of rounds of bingo, a Sub-Lieutenant's wife calling out the numbers in a dull monotone, before breaking for frothy instant coffee and stale shortbread. I was sat in the furthest corner of the room, desperately wishing the world would end so I wouldn't have to spend another second there, when I heard a faint rasping behind me and I turned to see one of the women hovering directly behind me. 'Lesley,' she barked, holding out her hand for me to shake, before adding, 'Warrant Officer's wife. So I take it your hubby just joined up? You being so young and all...' I smiled at her with as much enthusiasm as I could muster. 'He's at training at the moment. He's only been gone a week and I miss him so much already. I don't know how you ladies do it.' The Warrant Officer's wife nodded knowingly. 'Basic, huh? He called you yet?' I shook my head.

It was true I hadn't heard from Danny since I'd dropped him at the station, but I wasn't too worried. He'd warned me the first month would be tough and I expected he hadn't had a chance yet. 'No?' the woman said, her face suddenly contorting into a sour grin. 'Well don't count on it honey. Once he gets together with those boys he'll forget all about your skinny ass in about two seconds flat.' I felt my stomach lurch in protest. 'No, I don't think that's it at all...' I began, but the woman cut me off. 'Like a bunch of goddamned dogs they are, sniffing at the crack of any two-bit whore who crosses their path. When my Charlie got back he was so riddled with the clap it looked like his dick had rotted off...' I stood up and grabbed my bag, realising too late that the woman was obviously mad. 'But I still got on my knees and sucked it. And do you know why? Because I'm a goddamned patriot and that's my duty, you hear me lady?'

I backed away from her, my head spinning. 'Shut up! SHUT UP!' I screamed, the other women all turning to stare at me now. 'Oh give it a rest, Lesley,' someone yelled, before turning to me. 'Pay no attention to her, sweetie. She's just bitter that her husband upgraded to a younger, slimmer *model.' But the Warrant Officer's wife kept calling after me, even as I reached the door, her words ringing in my ears as I ran for the street. 'You think you're different honey? Special? He'll be just like all the others. You mark my word. Just you wait and see... '*

Just you wait and see.

* * *

Ever since I can remember I've had the same dream. Reccurrin sort of, 'cept it's not identical every time. Details change and shift around, but the main bits are all there. The bones. It always starts the same way. I'm walkin home from school. Now this is my first school you understand, from when I was around your age. I walked that route every goddamned day when I was a kid, and even though it's been twenty years since I've been back I still know every inch of it, like it's burnt into me or somethin.

For some reason it's always autumn. It's cold. Some people say they only dream in black and white, or without sound or smell or touch or taste. Not me though. I can see my breath billowin smoke-like against the grey-blue sky, feel the tingle of chilblains in my fingertips and toes. The road is varnished with a mush of dead leaves, oranges and reds, yellows and browns. There's not a dog turd in sight. I said it was vivid, not realistic ha.

I'm with three or four of my friends. Well, I guess they're my friends. I can't see their faces for the complicated arrangements of home-knitted balaclavas and scarves that coil around their necks and shoulders. For some reason in my dream I'm never wearing a hat or scarf. No gloves neither. My hands are the colour of rare steak. We're walkin pretty slowly. Meanderin like, as if we ain't got no place better to be, despite the weather. You noticin a theme here son? Always with the walkin, awake or asleep. What I wouldn't give jus' for once to have a dream where I'm sat on a bus or a train – a goddamned horse even. Jus' so my poor legs could take a load off for a while. As we drift along I listen to my friends talkin. They're all deep in conversation, though I never quite manage to catch the thread of what they're sayin, their voices muffled and weirdly out of sync with each other. In the end I jus' nod along and laugh in the gaps. I guess 'cos it's a dream or whatever no one stops to point out that I look like a total dick.

The road we're on seems to go on forever and ever, and one by one my friends start to peel off, wavin goodbye and yellin things in their strange distorted voices until finally I'm left alone. That's when I see the man. He's standin on the other side of the road with his back turned to me. He's wearing a hat and smokin a cigarette, so that from behind it looks like the top of his head is on fire. I think I recognise him. He's roughly the same height and build as my own father – your granddaddy, God rest his soul. Somethin about his jacket is familiar too, a long, old-fashioned trench coat, loosely belted at the hip. I think I remember playin dress-up in it as a kid, pretendin I was a detective or somethin. Damn fine coat it was. Mum used to say it made him look like a movie star. I remember baggin it up and throwin it out with the rubbish ten years later once the bottle finally got the better of the ol' man.

Suddenly the guy across the road starts runnin. Jus' bolts off, back in the direction I came from. Well naturally I start runnin too, chasin after him as he abruptly veers off the main street and starts down some winding alley that I've never seen before and which I suspect doesn't really exist. Still I keep runnin. It's weird, no matter how fast I pump my legs I never seem to gain any distance on him. He's always nine or ten steps ahead of me, his coat whippin out behind him, his face forever hidden from view. Eventually the alley yawns open to reveal a large clearin, a deserted green field fringed by trees on three sides. The man moves to the centre of the field and stops dead on the spot, still keepin his back to me. I stop too, my heart poundin in my chest, my lungs screamin, a sense of dread risin in me now. Because I know what is about to happen.

Because it happens like this every time.

Slowly the man begins to twist, pivotin at the waist so that the lower half of his body is still facin forwards. And everythin is plunged into ultra slow-motion, a bead of sweat on my forehead frozen mid-trickle, the wings of a nearby fly slowed from a blur to a beat. And still the man turns.

And if you were watchin me sleep son, you'd know I'd reached this part of the dream because I'd start thrashin my arms and kickin my legs and whimperin and moanin. I know I do it – your mother told me so.

And still the man turns. I want to run but I can't. I want to scream but I can't. And the man keeps turnin until he is facing me and finally I can see what he is hidin under his hat. And it ain't my daddy's face. Ain't no Monster's face neither.

In fact, it ain't no face at all.

Right under the brim of his hat is a shimmerin flat surface reflectin the sky, dazzlin white. A mirror.

I try to run again, but my legs are still rooted to the spot and I end up tumblin to the floor. That's when my fingers brush up against a large jagged rock. And right then I know exactly what I have to do. Slowly climbin to my feet, my whole body shakin with fear, I take one last look at the weird mirror-faced guy and launch the rock as hard as I can at his head.

The moment the rock leaves my fingers everything slows down again and I watch as it loops through the sky towards him, its trajectory perfect, odds-on for a direct hit. Suddenly, when the rock is no more than a coupla millimetres away from him, the man shifts his weight so that for the first time he is lookin straight at me.

And of course it is my face I see, reflected back in the silver glass. And I know then that I've made a mistake.

But it's too late.

The rock hits and the man explodes, not just his face but his body too, shatterin into a billion shards that glisten in the air for a moment before fallin to the floor.

I look around the clearin, empty now except for the small pile of glass, and spot for the first time what looks like a field of yellow flowers in the distance, a smudge of sunshine amongst the endless grey and green. I start runnin towards it, tryin to shake the image of the man from my head, until finally I reach the edge of the field. And it's not flowers, but maize, the tall crops swayin high over my head. Seven, eight feet high. Dwarfin me. And no matter how old I am in the dream, I always feel like a child. I reach out to grab an ear of corn, the split pod more like a mouthful of rotten teeth than any ear I've ever seen. I let go of the corn, and then without thinkin I dive into the field, partin the thick stems and chargin forwards so that within a couple of seconds I am completely disorientated, only small fragments of sky visible between the mass of green above me. I keep runnin, faster and faster, changin direction on a whim, zigzaggin through the neatly planted rows, going deeper and deeper.

And then suddenly I stop. Just like that. I stop and I sink to my knees as if I am about to cry, or pray. But I do neither. I do nothin but kneel, happy to be lost, cocooned amongst the corn. And I wait there, countin the seconds until it is time to wake up.

* * *

Ever since I can remember I've had the same dream. Well, at least I have since Daddy died. It's difficult to remember what my dreams were like before then. Quite often I forget I've had it until much later. 'Waking a dream', my mother used to call it. You'll be going about your day, minding your own business, when all of a sudden there will be some innocuous trigger – you'll turn and catch your reflection in a shop window, or notice the severe tone of a stranger disciplining his dog – and then it will all come rushing back to you, like déjà vu, or the melody to some long-forgotten song, a spotlight shining on the darkest corners of the night. And you'll remember everything.

I wake up. That's how it starts, though of course I am not really awake. It's like I have two sets of eyelids and I've only opened one of them. I'm still dreaming, only I don't know it yet. As far as I'm concerned it's just any other day. *I look around my room (which, thanks to dream-logic, is always my bedroom in my parents' house, no matter how old I am) and everything looks perfectly safe and normal. Everything is just as it should be. I get out of bed and stretch and yawn, go to the bathroom, and then go downstairs for breakfast. And that's when things cease to make sense.*

My mum is frying eggs at the stove when I walk into the kitchen, and she doesn't notice me at first. I try to speak and say good morning to her but my throat feels tight and raw. Sometimes when I dream, everything will be vague and abstract – more feelings than a fully-realised head-movie. This dream though is ultra-vivid and hyper-realistic, the colours rich and saturated, every sense fully realised. I can smell the eggs bubbling in extra-virgin olive oil; I can taste the after-tang of toothpaste on my tongue. And I can feel the spasm of fear in the deepest recesses of my being as my mum turns around to wish her darling daughter good morning.

And then starts screaming her fucking head off.

Confused, I hold up my hands and try to speak, to ask her what's wrong, but my throat is still sore and the sound that comes out is more like: 'Grrrrroooaaarrrr!' I watch as Mum backs away in terror, reaching for the pan and flinging it in my direction, splattering me with splashes of scalding oil, the egg hurtling through the air and landing with a wet plop on the floor between us. For a second I glance at the egg, something about its appearance simultaneously absurd and tragic, before I am distracted by a loud CLANG! and I look up to see Mum has climbed up onto the kitchen surface and is now aiming various kitchen appliances in my direction, at the same time screaming for my dad to fetch his gun.

Diving out of the way of a flying toaster, I scramble towards the back door and hurl myself through, yelling for help myself now, trying to tell the world that my mum has gone crazy – that she's trying to kill me! Over the fence I spot the shadow of old Mrs Cole (this is the same Mrs Cole who, like my dad, has been dead for more than a decade, a fact that for whatever reason never registers in my dream) and I start sprinting towards her. 'Grrrrroooaaarrrr!' I say, desperately trying to explain to her that my life is in danger. However, it seems old Mrs Cole is also uninterested in my plight, and next thing I know she is brandishing an electric hedge trimmer and threatening to slice my face off if I take one more step in her direction.

I spin around and start running the opposite way, hurdling over garden fences with surprising ease, occasionally encountering a neighbour, who either runs away or tries to kill me, or both, until finally I make it out of the suburbs and into the city centre, where of course I am confronted by a catalogue of disaster movie clichés: cars crashing into fire hydrants, police helicopters circling overhead, while all around people scream and run at the sight of me. Oh, and it's now inexplicably night.

It's normally at this point that I start to wonder if I might be dreaming. It's a difficult call. Everything seems so unlikely and backwards, and yet... well, how many times does life seem unlikely and backwards – impossible even – but then it turns out you are actually awake? How many times have you turned on the news and thought, this can't be happening?

This can't be real.

As a stampede of heavily armed riot police begin charging towards me, I decide it's probably for the best if I don't stick around to find out.

Bounding over burnt-out cars, I dive deeper into the city, tumbling headfirst into the rubble, picking myself up and dusting myself down then falling over again, my body tiring from the endless chase, when suddenly I spot salvation. Rising up out of the dust and smoke is a giant, silver skyscraper, like a vertical river flowing endlessly up towards the sky. Switching direction, I head for the entrance, ducking low to avoid the beams of searchlights that have begun to arc through the night, until finally I reach the door.

Which is naturally locked.

I leap up towards an open window, desperately trying to get a hold of something so I can begin to scale the building King Kong-like. All the while the wail of sirens is growing louder, mingling in with the buzz of rotor blades, the crackle of megaphones: Stop where you are! We have you surrounded! There is no chance of escape!

And I keep jumping but the ledge is just out of reach, until eventually it dawns on me that I am not going to make it. Because I am not a giant ape stolen from an unexplored tropical paradise, I'm a human being…

Aren't I?

And here the dream lurches towards its tragic TV-movie twist, an imaginary camera panning out to provide a full out-of-body experience.

And I am expecting fangs.

Claws.

Scales.

Webbed feet?

But actually, I see nothing of the sort. All I see is a scared little girl, surrounded by an angry mob and an armed response unit. And as the helicopter lands, the searchlight illuminating the hordes who have cornered me, their guns drawn, their pitchforks flaming, I finally glimpse the faces of my killers.

And I am surrounded by Monsters.

Once, a few months before we were married, I tried to tell Danny about my dream. We were lying in bed one morning, when he started telling me about this crazy reoccurring nightmare he'd just had, about his dad being made of glass or something. I told him I had something similar.

'Hang on,' he said after I finished. 'So everyone else had turned into a Monster apart from you?' I nodded. 'Everyone except Mum and Mrs Cole, unless they changed later. Weird huh?' Danny thought for a while. 'Y'know if everyone else in the world turns into a Monster except for you, then I think that still makes you *a Monster.'*

I frowned.

'I don't know if it works like that… ' Danny sat up. 'Sure it does. That's fuckin Einstein – the theory of relativity or whatever.' I shrugged, unconvinced. 'Anyway, even if I did turn into a Monster – if you woke one morning and I had a green head and a long tail – what would you do? I'd still be me wouldn't I?' Danny grinned and rolled on top of me. 'Well… ' he said.

I guess I'd take my gun and shoot you right in the middle

of your ugly fuckin head.
BLAM!
Just to make sure.
Ha.

Two

Long story short we was dyin. And I don't mean that as no metaphor. I mean we was actually dyin. As in we didn't have enough water in our bodies to sustain life for much longer. I'm talkin hours, not days. Cal looked like shit, his eyes raw and bloodshot, his arms hangin loosely by his sides. Jim too looked like he was ready to drop, and I wasn't doin much better myself, the pebble I'd slipped under my tongue havin long stopped doin its job. My ears were ringin and my head was poundin, every step a dull mallet blow to my skull. I'd slowed down too, the momentum gone from my legs, each step like wadin through a swamp.

I knew the end wouldn't be long.

We'd left the empty village before sunrise and headed in a straight line. I don't think any of us really believed we were goin to make it to the airstrip anymore. Walkin was just a way of distractin ourselves from the inevitable. In the end I guess it's all we knew how to do. Puttin one foot in front of another. In front of another. Even for the desert, the heat was bad, the sun seemin to have developed a personal vendetta against us. Really stickin the knife in.

All of us except Jim were down to our vests by now, to hell with the sunburn. This was our fourth day without washin and I don't mind tellin ya, we smelt bad. Stank. Especially Doggie. I spent the day walkin upwind to the fat fuck and more than once I thought about puttin a bullet in his head and leavin him for the crows. I ain't kiddin. He had that fuckin kitten back with him too, pokin out the top of his vest like a joey in a pouch. Can't have had much of a sense of smell or it wouldn't have stayed in there for long ha. Goddamn thing never stopped mewlin for a second. I decided I'd put a bullet in its head too.

Jett was another one. Don't get me started on *him*. I swear to god that kid's got more beans than fuckin Heinz. There we were, draggin our sorry carcasses through the sand – burnt, dehydrated, slowly starvin to death – and there was Bobby Boy Scout, hoppin all over the place like a goddamned cocker spaniel on heat. One minute he's scramblin up a sand dune to gauge our position, the next he's stooped over yellin to anyone who'll listen how he's found a set of Monster tracks. 'So what if you have?' I croaked when I finally caught up with him. The kid shook his head a few times, fuckin epileptic with excitement. 'But shouldn't we, y'know, document them? So we can let command know…' I looked down at the small scuff marks in the sand, as likely caused by a tumbleweed as anything else, and then back at Jett. 'Oh *sure!*' I said, a great big smile stretchin across my face. 'Wait while I fetch my camera.' I fumbled for my fly, unzippin and floppin my tackle out. And then, with enormous effort, I managed to squeeze out what must've been the last five or six drops of piss left in my entire body. 'There ya go!' I said as I shook her off. 'All nice and documented. I can't wait for the Commander to read my report.'

This was how it'd been for days now, snappin at each other like a bunch of bitches. Of course, the meds don't help. You see son, when they first sent us out here no one really had any idea about the kind of threats we faced. Still don't. Of course the papers go on about people gettin eaten and shit, but the truth is that even after all this time we still don't have a goddamned clue what these Monsters are capable of. Might they shoot laser beams out of their eyes? Or fireballs out of their arseholes? Honestly we don't know.

That's where the meds come in.

The army, erring on the side of caution, decided to dose us up against every fuckin malady known to man. We've had jabs for measles and botulism, chicken pox and anthrax, and that's before we get into the pills. We got red ones for depression, green ones for fatigue, purple ones for malaria and blue ones for I don't know what. To keep our peckers hard? Ha. Must be twenty a day we're supposed to take in all. I ain't kiddin – I near enough rattle when I walk! The worst thing's the side effects. Can't shit for a week the first time ya start takin 'em, nor when you stop neither. Then there's the dry mouth, twitches, dizziness, blurred vision – basically you wake up with the worst hangover of your life every single fuckin mornin.

Anyway when the campsite was sacked we lost nearly all the medical supplies along with everythin else, so the last few days we've all been comin down like motherfuckers. I swear, I've been hallucinatin all kinds of crazy shit. Yesterday I happened to look down and instead of a seeing a pair of suede desert boots there was a pair of hooves poking out the bottom of my combats. Hooves! Two pointy black toes sproutin from a shrub of brown fur. I looked like Mr-fuckin-Tumnus! I even spotted a perfect set of prints windin out behind me as far as I could see, each track like an upside-down heart, split in two. I blinked a coupla times and looked down again. The hooves stayed where they was. Fuck it, I thought. At least I hadn't grown a tail.

Of course Jett's unremittin perkiness made the comedown about a thousand times worse. I watched him ziggin and zaggin this way and that, grinnin like a special needs kid in a cake shop. Doggie too was a little too upbeat for my likin. He'd started singin to the cat now, some fuckin homo RnB crap or somethin, kinda shit your mother used to start screechin when she'd got one too many shooters in her, only Doggie probably had a better voice ha. *'You are beautiful... '* I ain't kiddin – and this is to the cat! Christ, there I was with barely enough energy left in me to swat the flies that festered around my eyes and mouth, like one of those god damned pot-bellied African kids from the AIDS commercials, and those two were actin as if they'd just got back from a week's R&R in Aruba. Nah. It wasn't right.

Then I had a thought. Those fuckers had water. That was it. They must've stashed a bottle back at the camp. Or maybe they found somethin at the village and kept it for themselves. Didn't Jett say something about findin a well? Those sons of bitches! I pictured them sneakin off together, laughin as they splashed their faces and spittin out what they didn't need – silver droplets glistenin in the air, disappearin forever the second they hit the sand. Well, it was too much to take. I started to lift my rifle, my finger fumblin for the trigger. I'd take out those double crossin bastards if it were the last thing I ever did.

And that's when I saw it. For a second I thought it was another hallucination, a mirage or whatnot, but then Cal started yellin, then Doggie and Jim and Jett – even me – all of us whoopin and screamin like children. And then we were runnin, the rifle fallin from my hand as I sprinted forwards, my anger forgotten. Because no matter how impossible it seemed, stretched out not 500 yards in front of us, was a lake.

* * *

After the disaster of the Military Spouses Meet-Up Club I decided it would be safer to spend some time at home. Danny would be back in a month, and until then I had plenty to be getting on with in the apartment. I wanted to redecorate the bedroom – not because of anything the crazy Warrant Officer's wife had said about duty or being a patriot – just, well Danny was my husband and I wanted to make things nice for him when he got home. And besides, before he left we'd been talking about having

A baby.

The days fluttered by and the apartment began to take

shape; not just the bedroom but the bathroom, kitchen, living room – the whole place painted and furnished courtesy of Mum's life insurance policy – until finally every room was fresh and new and clean and I was forced to admit to myself that I was finished. All in all it had taken me three weeks, meaning I still had a week left before Danny was due back. That was, if he was still coming back. I'd still not heard anything from him since he'd left; no letter, no phone call, and no matter how many times I tried to convince myself I was being stupid, that I was a strong, independent woman in a healthy, trusting relationship

I was still scared.

With no one around I turned to my computer for reassurance, hanging around on military websites and recruitment forums to remind myself exactly what Danny was going through; the 5am starts, the 10km hikes, the cold showers, the endless assault courses, trying to work up some guilt to replace the resentment simmering in my stomach. However, it seemed every search I entered seemed to throw up more doubts: links to news reports of questionable interrogation techniques or fresh atrocities committed on foreign soil, or else the latest rampage by yet another psychotic soldier, not to mention the endless stream of anti-war blogs and conspiracy forums. In the end I turned the machine off, resolving to do something productive with my time instead.

But what?

The fact was I was bored. *Time seemed to have stopped altogether, the days stretching on endlessly as I trudged through hours of mindless daytime TV, the pictures and words slurring in and out of focus, the lack of human interaction finally starting to take its toll as I realised it had been weeks since I'd spoken to anybody.*

I felt like I was in a desert.

I tried to stay in bed for as long as possible in the morning and then went to bed early at night, sometimes even before it got dark, all the while making a superhuman effort to avoid the clock.

But it was no good.

By mid-week I found myself eyeing up the bottle of vodka that had stood on the kitchen side since Danny had left, wondering if it was too early to have a double with lunch. In the end I washed it away down the sink, not trusting myself not to finish it. And then buy another, and another. After that I just sat and waited, staring at the walls, dividing up the days into ever decreasing units of time left until I'd see Danny again; seventy-two hours, 4320 minutes, a quarter of a million or so seconds…

Until finally, there was a knock at the door.

I froze. After all this time apart I was suddenly unsure of myself. I'd already got dressed about fifteen times that morning, discarding dresses as too scruffy, or too slutty – or not slutty enough – applying and reapplying my make-up until I was certain everything was perfect. Yet now that he was actually here I found I was nervous, my stomach churning as if I was about to attend an interview rather than welcome my husband home. I took a deep breath, straightened my top and opened the door.

'Hey.'

Relief saturated my senses. He was back and he was smiling. Sure he looked tired, and crumpled and was that a… tattoo on his arm? But he was back. And just as handsome as I remembered – maybe even more so, the two-day stubble helping to define the jut of his jaw, his shoulders looking bigger and more welcoming than ever, even with the new eagle tattoo etched on his bicep. 'Hey,' he said again, squeezing past me into the apartment before I even had time to land a kiss on his cheek.

He stood there for a moment, blinking in the room. 'You… painted,' he said squinting at the walls. I nodded, suddenly self-conscious of my sloppy lines, worried I'd chosen the wrong colours. 'You like it?' I asked. Danny shrugged. 'Sure… I jus' wasn't expectin it is all… ' His accent seemed stronger. Rougher around the edges, as if he couldn't be bothered to finish his words anymore. An awkward silence seeped between us, like two strangers suddenly realising they had nothing in common beyond the weather. 'So... do you want something to eat?' I finally asked, swallowing down the drowning sensation, determined to stay afloat. 'You got steak?' Danny asked, a hint of excitement in his voice for the first time since he'd got home. I smiled. 'I've got bacon, gammon, sausage, ribs or chops.' Danny shrugged again. 'I ate on the plane.' I nodded, reminding myself that this was okay, that this was all normal behaviour. He was just trying to readjust to life on 'civvy-street'. I forced my smile even wider, watching as Danny dumped his bag and headed towards the bedroom. 'In fact I think I'm jus' gonna crash for a while. I'm beat.'

And with that he was gone.

The next two weeks were tougher than I ever could have imagined. Most days Danny was up at the crack of dawn, leaving me in bed while he ran circles around the block, or did one-handed push-ups in the kitchen. At breakfast he'd sit in silence, wolfing down a battery farm of eggs before immediately going back out to the gym for the rest of the day. It was crazy, like he was still in training or something. Like he couldn't switch off. Whenever I gently tried to suggest we did something together, like go to the cinema, or for a meal, or even for a walk, he swatted me away. It was his passing out parade in two weeks and he wanted to make sure he looked good for the photos. He only got one shot at it. It was important. Sure, I said. Of course. But the whole time I was thinking

What about me?

Worst of all was the lack of intimacy. I'm not just talking about sex, although a little wouldn't have hurt – Danny seeming to have lost all interest in that department since his return. No, what was hardest to take was the general lack of affection. I mean your father was never the most tactile of *people, but now it was like he went out of his way to avoid all physical contact with me, sleeping with his back to me at night, leaving the house for the gym each morning without so much as a peck on the cheek. And heaven forbid I actually tried to touch him…*

Still, it wasn't like he stayed out all night getting drunk. And he didn't beat me or call me names. To be fair, there were plenty of things he did *do well. DIY for example. And he kept the place unbelievably tidy, vacuuming the entire apartment at least three times a day. I had a lot to be grateful for. And who knew, once he'd officially passed out maybe things would settle down a bit and go back to the way they were before? Until then I figured I'd just sit tight and do my best to keep smiling and try my best to be a good wife.*

To do my duty.

Eventually the day of the parade arrived. Danny was in a great mood, nervous but excited, and looking stunning in his starched white gloves and black beret. Seeing as he didn't have anyone else to bring along I decided to invite my sister, who flew in especially that morning, leaving the girls behind. The ceremony wasn't due to take place until the afternoon, and while Danny stayed at home getting ready, my sister and I spent the morning shopping and catching up.

I hadn't seen her since Mum's funeral and to my surprise she was in high spirits. The girls were doing well at school, she'd gone back to work and she'd even started seeing someone. 'So what's he like?' I asked as we squeezed into a changing room together. 'Oh he's sweet and kind and he has a great sense of humour,' she blushed, before quickly adding, 'Of course, he's no action hero like Danny.' I grinned feebly, feeling for the first time since I was eight years old a pang of sibling rivalry. 'Oh my God don't do it sis!' I suddenly yelled, pointing at the elegant black dress she was mid-way through wriggling into. 'Seriously, it shows off your curves in all *the wrong places… '*

The actual parade was over much quicker than I'd

anticipated. There was a short ceremony at the beginning where the soldiers lined up together to salute the League of Peace flag while a senior officer read out their pledge to protect and enforce security throughout the world, after which we all trailed outside to watch the new recruits drill through formations as a military band pounded out a strident march. I scanned the jungle of feather plumes and red sashes to look for Danny, but everybody looked so similar in their uniforms it was impossible to make him out. I quickly grew bored of looking and instead turned my attention to the crowd, scanning the faces of the other wives and mothers to see if there was anyone I recognised.

There must have been a hundred people watching, each of them craning their necks to try and catch a glimpse of their loved one on their special day. The thing that struck me most was how happy everybody looked, their eyes glistening with genuine pride as they watched their men – and it was all men – out there on the square. After a while I began to feel guilty. The truth was, I was left a little cold by it all. I mean, sure it was nice to see Danny dressed up so nicely. Jeez, it was nice to see him for more than five minutes in one sitting. I just thought the whole thing would be a bit more personal. *After all, Danny had just more or less promised his life to the army:*

For richer or poorer.

For better or worse.

Yet what had the army promised him in return? The right to be one of a hundred other marching toy soldiers, saluting the flag over and over again.

Until death… ?

And even as the band trailed off and the boys fell in line for a final roll call, I looked out over the crowd and could see the next group of new recruits patiently waiting their turn to pass out, having presumably already finished with their pledges and promises. I suddenly found myself wondering how many other soldiers had already been out there before us today. A thousand? Ten thousand? More? Maybe the ceremony just went on continuously, twenty-four hours a day, 365 days a year – an endless factory production line pumping out identical batch-made soldiers, an entire army of Dannys, all of them marching away from me...

An old woman nudged me, grinning wildly. 'Wow, you must be so proud!'

I smiled back, my cheeks hurting with the effort, before turning to my sister. 'I need to get a drink. Now.*'*

Once the parade had finished we were led through to the 'grand hall' for the reception. It would be the first chance I'd had to actually talk to Danny – that was if I could spot him amongst the muddle of berets and boots, the huge room shrunken by the number of newly inaugurated servicemen, most of whom seemed to be growing increasingly loud as the trays of free drinks were emptied, replaced and then emptied again. As I handed a glass of sparkling wine to my sister and then grabbed one for myself, I began scouring the room for Danny, squeezing between young couples posing for photographs and mother-in-laws queuing for the bathroom until finally I spotted him, propped up against the bar next to a couple of other young-looking soldiers, a drink in each hand.

Laughing his head off.

'Hey,' I said as I sidled up to him. 'I was looking for you.' Danny smiled stupidly. He'd never been much of a drinker and already his eyes looked soft and unfocused. 'Sorry babe,' he said, sliding a muscular arm around the neck of the soldier stood next to him. 'You know how it is when I get together with the boys.' I nodded and knocked back my wine, reaching across him to pluck another from a passing waiter. 'So this is your wife, huh Dan?' said the soldier in the headlock, letting his gaze creep down my body to rest on my legs. 'You never said she was a honey! Aren't you going to introduce me?' Danny responded by giving him a quick jab in the kidneys. 'Lorna, this jackass you see before you is Private Schmitt...'

'Schwarz!' the soldier corrected him. 'Whatever. You don't need to worry about this Kraut fuckwit. He ain't gonna last long in the field – he's got the common sense of a fuckin cockroach!' Schwarz winked at me. 'Which coincidentally is the only thing that'll survive a nuclear holocaust... Speaking of which, how are you two celebrating your last few days together before we head off to face certain annihilation. I bet you've got a hotel room booked, huh? Let me guess, the Love Bird Suite?'

I glanced at Danny, searching his face for answers, finding nothing but pursed lips and a blank stare. Schwarz looked from Danny to me then back again before exploding into a fit of high-pitched laughter. 'You bastard!' he cackled. 'You absolute cocksucker – you haven't told her yet?' I reached out and grabbed Danny by the wrist, shaking his limp arm. 'Told me what?' Schwarz shook his head, still laughing. 'I mean, that's cold man. You haven't told her? Shit... ' I kept shaking, ignoring my sister's hand on my back, silently begging me to keep calm. 'What's he talking about Danny? What haven't you told me?'

And then finally, as if only just noticing me, he turned and grinned.

'Y'know I was gonna tell ya tonight baby. I wanted it to be a surprise but Schmitt here had to go and and open his fuckin pie-hole, didn't ya?'

The room roared with excitement and pride and the good cheer only unlimited complimentary drinks can bring.

'I was gonna tell ya. I'm serious... '

And somewhere behind me my sister held her breath.

'We got the call. A week ago. I'm startin my first tour of duty... '

The room fell silent, everyone turning to look at me. Even Schwarz had stopped laughing.

'I leave in a week.'

* * *

It was early evenin when we arrived at the lake, but that didn't stop us from divin straight into the water. I mean it, boots, packs, everythin – we just jumped right in fully clothed and started splashin around. Like kids in a swimming pool we were, climbin onto each other's shoulders and belly floppin back in, somersaultin underwater or usin our hands to spray each other. 'Course I've never drank so much in all my life. Gulped it down 'till I couldn't swallow another drop, 'till it felt like my belly would burst. After that I jus' lay there, floatin face down like a corpse, the cool water swishin around my teeth and tongue, my feet not touchin the floor.

The funny thing about the place was that it looked almost exactly like your paintin. I mean it, right down to the row of palm trees that bowed down over the water. It looked like we found ourselves a bona fide tropical paradise. Only thing we was missin was the sandcastles, ha.

It was completely dark by the time we scrambled out onto the bank, the cold night air instantly settin us shiverin. Cal was the first one to point out he was starvin. We all were. It's funny, only an hour earlier any one of us would've slit our own grandmother's throat for a half teaspoon of water, yet now that we'd had a drink all we could think about was how cold and hungry we were. I reckon we could've been sat at the swankiest restaurant in town with a plate full of pie, a bar full of beer and a hooker on each lap and we'd still be complainin that the chair was uncomfortable. But I guess that's what bein human is all about, huh?

As we peeled off our wet clothes we carved out a simple plan – Jim, Jett and Doggie would do a quick search of the surroundin area to see if they could forage anythin to eat while Cal and I would stay put and attempt to start a fire. I weren't holdin my breath on any food turnin up. Then again, I reminded myself as I wrung a river of water from my top, stranger things have happened.

It took a surprisingly short amount of time to get the fire going, the surrounding scrub providin decent enough kindlin.

We even managed to dig out an old stump that we found near the edge of the water and set it in the centre of the blaze. I swear, it was like someone upstairs was keepin an eye on us for once.

As we sat warmin ourselves over the flames, I happened to look up and see two fat, juicy coconuts high in the tree above us, danglin like a big ol' hairy pair of balls, jus' *askin* to be plucked. I gave Cal a nudge and pointed up. 'Look,' I said. 'Dinner.'

Now, I don't know how many trees you've climbed in your life, what with us livin in the city and all. Plus I've seen the way your mother is about health and safety and all that lefty shit. Jesus, she probably considers tree climbin an act of vandalism, an affront to the tree's incontrovertible rights or whatnot. Anyway, when I was your age I used to climb a shit load of trees. I'm serious, I pretty much lived in 'em – had my own tree house that I used to sleep in and everythin. Like a little monkey I was, shimmyin to the top, swingin from branch to branch. No one was better than me. Or quicker.

Thing is, back home the trees I used to climb were all ash, oak, chestnut. That sorta thing. Great wide jobs, with plenty of nooks to use as handholds and branches to swing a leg over. What I never practiced climbin though was no palm trees. Not even once. Shit, you ever seen a palm tree son? Great tall, skinny things they are, just one long pole disappearin way off over your head. Nowhere at all to get a grip. And the bark, Christ. It's like razor wire. I ain't kiddin!

After the first few tries Cal's hands were chewed up pretty bad, so I shoved him out the way and took a run up myself. By wrappin my vest round my hands I managed to crawl up maybe nine or ten feet before I missed my footin and slipped, scrapin my belly raw on the fall back to earth. 'Goddamned tree!' I snapped as I picked myself up off the dirt. 'If only we had some rope I could try and arrange a harness and… shit. I don't know.' I peered up at the coconuts. They seemed to be bobbin slightly in the flickerin light, tauntin us. I turned to

Cal to see if he had any ideas. 'Why don't we jus' shoot the fuckers down?' he shrugged. I shook my head dismissively, then stopped. It wasn't a bad idea. 'Ya reckon ya can hit 'em?' I asked. Cal lifted his gun. 'I reckon.' I took a step back, keepin a careful eye on the top of the tree to see where the fruit landed.

There was a loud CRACK! followed by a sizzle as both coconuts exploded. 'You fuckin idiot!' I yelled at Cal as he wiped tiny white shards from his face. 'Where the fuck did you learn to shoot? Waco?' Cal gave a small shrug and looked at his feet. 'Sorry.' I stared at the small pieces of shell that had landed in the fire, the husks already glowin orange in the flames. 'Forget it.' Jus' then there was a rustlin behind us and we turned to see a small bundle of fur emerge from the bushes.

It was Doggie's kitten.

It was another hour before Jim, Jett and Doggie returned from their foragin trip. They hadn't managed to find anythin except for a small handful of berries that Doggie was proudly holdin up for us all to see. Jim and Jett looked weary, their clothes still wet from the swim earlier. They perked up a little though when they saw the fire we'd built, and we shifted round to make space for 'em to sit down.

We waited until they'd dried off before we brought it out. Doggie handed out his berries – everyone got four – and we sat there chewin in silence. They tasted like mud and poison. 'Okay, fuck this,' I said, standin up and tossin my remainin three berries in the fire. 'Hey, what the hell d'ya think you're doin soldier?' Jim yelled. That's when I got up and fetched the meat from out the bushes, already washed and skinned with a stick shoved right through it. There was a stunned silence. And then the cheerin started. While it was cookin we told them the story of the coconuts, explained how after Dirty Harry here had finished blastin 'em to smithereens we'd heard a noise in the bushes and found a big ol' bird flappin around. 'You're lucky ya didn't let Cal loose on it,' said Jett.

'Else we'd be havin shredded duck for dinner.'

Everyone laughed.

Twenty minutes later we all sat lickin our fingers and wipin our chins. 'So what kind of bird was it again?' Doggie asked as he hacked himself yet another slither of flesh from the skewered lump of meat resting next to the fire. I sensed Cal starin across at me, tryin to catch my eye. 'A big 'un,' I answered with a grin.

'A real big 'un.'

After we finished up eatin we sat around talkin some more, pickin the meat from our teeth and tellin stories, talkin about scrapes we'd gotten ourselves into and whatnot. I guess I was feelin pretty good, because I piped up about a little trouble I had a few weeks back.

I was out on patrol with a few of the lads, just mindin our own business, when we see this thing comin over the horizon. I mean, it was fuckin horrible – eight legs, two heads – like nothing I've ever seen before, not in no classification guide, nothin. Jus' awful it was. So of course we start blastin away, sprayin it with lead until this thing drops to the floor, dead. Well that was easy, I thought, as we headed over towards it. We still had our guns out mind – I've seen too many horror movies in my time to start gettin sloppy – but as it turns out we didn't need 'em. 'Cos when we got a little closer I saw what it was we killed. Lyin on the floor was two camels, with what looked like four or five goatskins stretched over them. And behind the camels, three natives – blood seepin from their mouths, turnin their beards red.

I mean, I guess they were off to the market or whatever to sell the goat hides – but seriously? What the fuck did they think would happen, goin around like that? Of course they wound up getting shot. A couple of the guys got out their phones and started takin pictures. One of them, Macky, even took a piss on 'em. That Macky – he's always been a prick. We talked about buryin 'em but in the end we thought it best to jus' leave it to the crows. You can't get mixed up in that tribal shit, no siree.

When I finished talkin, nobody said anythin for a while.

Finally Jett cracked a grin. 'You know when you hear things like that… Well, I guess you could say it really gets my goat.'

Shit we did laugh.

Eventually the fire started to die and we started to think about turnin in. When Doggie got up to go for a piss I noticed that Cal had passed out in the dirt. I turned to Jett and asked if he had a blanket or something we could chuck over him. That's when Jim decided to stick his nose in. 'Private Marshall needs to wake his ass up this instant. We're in an unknown location and it's vital we secure the perimeter overnight. I've drawn up a rota so… '

I didn't wait for him to finish. 'Now wait a minute, Jim. It's been a hell of a few days in case you haven't noticed. Starvation, dehydration, sunburn. We're fucked. All of us. You're fucked Jim, just look at yourself. Don't ya think it might be worth havin a night off? To recuperate I mean.' Across the remains of the fire Jett was starin at us. Unusually for Jett, he seemed reluctant to take sides. I guess he wanted some sleep too. Jim was insistent though. 'Do you think Monsters take a night off, soldier? Well, do you? Because at the end of the day they're the reason why we're in this shit. They don't take a night off. Not a second. Now perhaps if the perimeter had been a little more secure a couple of nights back then things wouldn't have gone down the way they did. And would you please address me as Staff Sergeant… '

Well son, I ain't proud but at this point I have to admit I may have lost my temper some with the commandin officer. In fact, as my ol' daddy used to say, I gave it to him with both barrels.

'Now you listen to me, *Jim*. We ain't goin to secure the perimeter. It ain't happenin. Not tonight, anyway. The boys here need sleep, so I say we let them sleep. If you want to go then be my guest. But I'll tell ya this for nothin, ya ain't gonna see no Monsters. Ya wanna know why? Because there ain't none!'

Opposite me I sensed Jett freeze. I knew I'd gone too far, but what could I do? I couldn't back down now. I carried on, warmin to my subject. 'I mean it – when's the last time we had a confirmed sightin? Eight years? Nine? Who knows, maybe they were here once, a long time ago, but they're sure as shit gone now. That's why we're bein sent home. Nah, the only attacks we gotta worry about are from mosquitoes. Them and the wogs. And who can blame 'em, huh? Maybe if we spent a bit more time buildin roads instead of stealin their oil… '

I didn't know where it was all comin from, these words. Hangin round with your mother too long probably. Fillin my head with her bullshit. All I knew was that I was angry. Angry and tired.

Jim leapt to his feet. 'That's *enough* soldier! It's one thing havin you disobey a direct order. That I can put down to exhaustion, or maybe jus' plain old fashioned retardedness. But what I *will not* tolerate is havin you disrespect the memory of every man, woman and child who has died in this conflict by spoutin out some *damn commie hogwash* to anyone who'll listen… ' He was jabbin his finger at me, his fury silhouetted against the night sky. 'Now in the interest of the group I will not address this issue formally until we make our way back to base, but rest assured when we do return I will ensure that your comments are properly documented and passed on to the appropriate authorities, who will no doubt give you the opportunity to explain your theories in much greater detail. Until that point however, I would be grateful if you would keep your revolting opinions to yourself. *Do I make myself clear?*'

I looked across at Jett and Cal, who was now rubbin the sleep from his eyes. Neither of them would catch my eye. 'Yes sir,' I mumbled.

'Good. Patrol commences from 2100 hours. Private

Marshall and I will take the first watch with a handover every two hours from then until daybreak.' And with that he was gone, marching off into the night, followed by a confused-lookin Cal. We sat in silence for another few minutes until we heard a crashin in the bushes and looked up to see Doggie, a look of concern etched on his stupid face.

'Hey, has anyone seen Lucky?'

That night none of us got much sleep. Instead we carried out the patrol exactly as Jim'd requested, swappin every two hours to take our turns walkin in circles in the dark, not one of us seein a damn thing worth mentionin. While I was out there I made my mind up to talk to Jim. I might have overstepped the mark, but there was no need for him to speak to me like that. I wanted to let him know that I thought he was bein a jerk for no good reason, and that his attitude wasn't gonna help any of us in the long run. I weren't gonna get angry, jus' spell it out to him plain and simple in a way he couldn't argue with. Yeah, I had a whole little speech planned out in my head.

In the end though I never had a chance to use it. Because by the time the sun finally rose in the east and the sky cracked blister blue and red, Jim was already dead.

* * *

Danny was gone again – although as I ghosted around the spotless apartment I found myself wondering whether he'd ever been there at all. The first few days following the passing out parade I'd refused point blank to speak to Danny, barricading him from the bedroom and forcing him to sleep on the sofa while he made half-hearted grovelling noises in my direction. To be honest I'd almost enjoyed it. After all, it was the most attention I'd had since he'd got back.

As I drove my sister to the airport we studiously avoided the topic of my faltering marriage, talking about the kids, her job, her new man – anything but Danny. Still, I couldn't help noticing the little concerned glances she kept shooting me across the car, or the little sigh she gave whenever she said my name.

'Oh Lorna... '

But whatever. My sister wasn't exactly in a position to talk when it came to tragic life stories, and as tempted as I was to jump on the plane with her and fly away from the carnage, I knew in my heart that I needed to stay and pick up the pieces. At the very least then I'd be able to see what I had.

And whether it was worth holding on to.

As the day of Danny's departure drew closer, he did his best to bridge the chasm that had opened up between us. The day before he was due to leave he came home with a bunch of flowers – the first I'd received in my married life – and that evening we sat down and ate dinner together. As I cut into the steak he'd cooked me, Danny set about trying to apologise again. 'Don't,' I said, cutting him off. 'All I'm asking for is a bit of communication. I mean – it's not like you're popping down the road for a pint of milk. How long are you going to be gone for again? Three months?' 'Six,' Danny mumbled. 'Six months! And you weren't even going to tell me?' Danny sat there chewing his steak. 'I'm sorry,' he said eventually. He said the words slowly, like he meant them.

It wasn't much.

But it was all I had.

That night we made love for the first time since he'd returned from training. It was rough, animal sex – angry, desperate – but it was good. Cathartic. And when we finally collapsed in a dehydrated heap a few hours later I knew I could never leave him. That he was as much a part of me as my leg, or my heart. I fell asleep and didn't dream.

In the morning we said goodbye at the door, having previously decided I wouldn't drive him to the station again, and then he was gone, walking down the hall, a small bag clutched under one arm. I was alone again. This time though, I was determined to take control of my life. If I was to be an army widow I wanted to at least fill my days with something worthwhile. Which is how, after a few weeks of fruitlessly searching through night school brochures and internet forums, I found myself volunteering as a shop assistant at my local branch of Save the Animals. The shop itself was something of a bombsite, with stacks of clothes strewn in no discernible order and random junk cluttering up every available inch of floor space; broken toys mingled in with stacks of vintage bodybuilding magazines, unspooling VHS cassettes tangled around crumbling boxes of Bakelite bangles. It would take a lifetime to sort it all out – which, seeing as I had nothing but time on my hands, suited me just fine.

On my third day there I was introduced to the new store manager, Dustin, who had recently transferred from another branch. 'Hmmm, recovering alcoholic or clinically unhappy cat lady?' he asked, watching as I attempted to sort a selection of loose pearl earrings from a tub of marbles. 'What, they're my only two choices?' I asked. 'How do you know I'm not a socially conscious billionairess?' Dustin grinned, 'Oh, I'm sorry – I'm afraid that's all we usually get in here. The mad, the sad and the bad. Still, it's always nice to make the acquaintance of a borderline-psychotic fantasist. Great to meet you.'

He was tall and good-looking in a nerdy, app-designer sort of way, sharply dressed in an open necked shirt and designer glasses, an expensive-looking smart watch strapped to his wrist. In fact, he was far too well dressed, too shiny and refined – next to the tatty chaos of Save the Animals he resembled a time-traveller from the future. I was instantly suspicious. 'Lorna,' I said, sticking out my hand. 'And what about you? Paedophile? Serial killer? Don't tell me – you're one of those men who still lives at home with Mummy and spends his evenings painting model tanks and planes?' 'Close,' he nodded. 'Except I don't live with my mum. But seriously, I'm just your run-of-the-mill, politically engaged, hybrid-driving, blog-reading, sushi-eating, loft-dwelling über asshole.' He smiled. 'Welcome to Save the Animals.'

Over the next few weeks Dustin and I formed an unholy alliance, terrorising the old women who visited the shop, playing tricks on each other and generally goofing off whenever we got the chance. It had quickly transpired that Dustin was both as pretentious and self-deprecating as his initial description of himself suggested, and to my surprise I found we had much in common. For one thing it was apparent that neither of us gave a shit about saving animals. No, the real reason we were both there was because we had nowhere else to go – or at least nowhere we wanted to be. Being something of a perpetual student, Dustin had more letters after his name than most CEOs, yet the thought of committing himself to a 'real' job filled him with dread. So instead he was happy to live on minimum wage and use and abuse his position to siphon off donations of rare and collectible vinyl records to sell on eBay for a profit.

For my part, I was running from Danny – or at least the reality of life without him. Not that I was willing to share any of my own miserable half-existence with Dustin. In fact, when on our second day working together he asked if I had a boyfriend, I point-blank denied Danny's existence altogether, having slid off my wedding ring and left it on the bathroom cabinet the day Danny left. It wasn't that I fancied Dustin – far from it. I guess I was just tired of dragging around all of the ridiculous baggage that came with being a soldier's wife. Besides, it felt good to be just plain old Lorna again, if only for eight short hours a day.

As before, I received no contact from Danny – no phone call to say he'd arrived safely, no letter lamenting how much he missed me – yet somehow, between my work at Save the Animals and my burgeoning friendship with Dustin, it all felt more manageable this time around. I began spending more and more time at the shop, volunteering for extra shifts at the weekend, doing anything I could to spend time away from the apartment, and all the unhappy memories it contained.

After around six weeks at Save the Animals, Dustin asked me if I'd like to meet him for a drink after work one night. My first response was one of panic – I still hadn't mentioned Danny to Dustin and I was worried about giving him the wrong impression. In addition to this, I'd been feeling out of sorts for the last couple of weeks. It was hard to put a finger on exactly what was wrong with me – a general malaise had coiled itself around me, and the thought of sharing a bottle of wine with Dustin actually turned my stomach. In the end though I felt I couldn't refuse. After all, Dustin was the first new friend I'd made since school, unless you counted Danny.

And I wasn't sure if I could *still count Danny.*

With that in mind, and promising myself I'd only stay for one short drink, I made my way across town on a dark and dreary Tuesday evening to meet Dustin, keeping my eyes open for an even darker and drearier bar.

The place he'd suggested we meet was called the Tokyo Lucky Hole, *a notorious downtown dive, popular with middle-class alcoholics and art-school poseurs. I'd been there once before actually, years ago, back when I was an alcoholic-poseur-student myself, and the sticky floors and stink of stale beer brought back embarrassing memories of dodgy dancing and drunken fumbles.*

'No, Steve – that's the whole point! They want *you to think that… '*

I heard Dustin before I saw him. He was propped against the bar with a beer in his hand, gesticulating at the barman. The volume of his voice told me it wasn't his first beer. 'Oh, hey Lorna,' he smiled as he spotted me, before turning back to the barman. 'Right then, you capitalist scumbag,' he said. 'Why don't you stop antagonising the punters and do your bloody job for once. What are you having, colleague? *Tequila slammer? Triple sambuca?' I smiled at the barman. 'Just a lemonade please.' Dustin thumped the bar. 'What? You drag me halfway across town to this* toilet *of a public house and you won't even have a real drink with me? That's just bad form, Lorn!' I shook my head and sighed. 'Okay, stick a vodka in there,' I said to the barman.* 'Single.'

'Friend of yours?' I asked as we took a seat in a grimy booth. 'Who Steve? Nah. I just like to shout politics at every member of the service industry I come across. It keeps them on their toes.' I laughed. It was reassuring to see that Dustin was as much of an immature, combative asshole in real life as he was at work – even if it did mean I had to spend every other breath telling him to shut up. But it was nice. Chilled. Just two colleagues – friends even – hanging out and having a drink after work. Totally normal. Completely legitimate. And 100%

Not a date.

For the next hour or so the world outside disappeared as I listened to Dustin tearing into everything from corporate tax avoidance to secret surveillance networks, only pausing to take increasingly large swallows of beer. I was taken aback. While I was used to his stream of conscious monologues from our time at work – nodding idly as he espoused the virtues of a rare Miles Davis recording or moaned about the launch of a new social network – here at the Tokyo Lucky Hole with three or four pints inside him he was transformed. Focused, furious; a one-man campaigning machine with facts at his fingertips and fire in his belly.

And what fire.

As he waved at Steve to bring over another round of drinks without breaking for breath, I noticed the damp patches under his armpits. He was actually sweating as he strained to connect an increasingly disparate set of global dots. Whether railing against illegal drilling in the Antarctic or radioactive dumping sites in Uruguay, he did seem to genuinely believe everything he was saying – although thankfully he was also self-aware enough to recognise how sickening his righteousness might seem, littering his rants with asides, such as: 'And I know *I'm a self-righteous dick, but... ' or 'For god's sake, there I go again... '*

While I just smiled and nodded and drank my drink.

'Mmmm.'

'Uh-huh.'

At some point Dustin got up and staggered to the toilet, leaving me in deafening silence for a couple of minutes. Even though I was still feeling guilty about Danny, I was forced to admit to myself I was having a good time. I guess it was just refreshing to hear somebody speak with passion about something – or at least to talk about anything *outside of television or work or shopping. To give the impression they were actually alive for once. Funnily enough, the only other person I'd heard speak like that before was Danny, when he was talking about the army.*

Except Danny only usually spoke about killing things.

As I was sitting there thinking, I happened to notice Dustin's jacket, which was hanging limply on the back of his chair. A leaflet of some sort was poking out of the pocket. And maybe I thought it was something to do with Save the Animals or maybe it was just because I'd had one too many vodkas or maybe I was just being a nosy bitch, but either way I reached across the table and tugged the little flyer and laid it flat on the table.

And I started to read:

Fuck The Fake War!

Next Sunday will see the thirteenth anniversary of Year Zero.

Thirteen years of lies and injustice.

Thirteen years of slime and sleaze.

Thirteen years of being told: mission accomplished.

1,000,000 civilians dead, 5,000 soldiers wounded – and still no Monsters.

Our planet choking, our economy unravelling – and still no Monsters.

How many more people have to die before we stand up and ask:

The leaflet went on, giving the details of a rally taking place next week, but before I could read any more I looked up and saw Dustin was on his way back to the table. I was still too shocked to even attempt to pretend I hadn't been snooping and so I just sat there, the glossy paper lying in front of me like a piece of evidence. 'So are you coming comrade?' Dustin asked with a grin.

Realising he wasn't pissed off at me for going through his pockets, my shock quickly began to evolve into resentment. 'Huh?' I spat, not bothering to look up. 'To the rally?' he continued. 'They say it's going to be the biggest since Year Zero. A million people on the street maybe – one for every murder by our boys in uniform.' I took a deep breath, counted to five.

And exploded.

'And what about all those murdered by Monsters, hmmm? Where's their march?' Dustin shrugged, on a roll now, oblivious to my rage. 'Oh pur-lease. Don't tell me you've fallen for all that government-sanctioned bullshit about the hidden 'enemy' in the sand? Who by the way always happen *to live in oil-producing nations? My, isn't that a happy accident… '*

Somewhere in the distance I heard the sound of breaking glass, followed by Steve swearing.

I stood up and punched Dustin as hard as I could.

'Fuck!'

Dustin was doubled over the table, clutching his face with both hands. 'You fucking hit me!'

I stood there shaking. A couple of people around me had stopped talking and turned to see what was going on. It might have looked like an 'edgy' downtown bar, but in reality it was just a façade – a place where middle-class white kids came to look tough, even as they sipped their bottles of organic craft beer. It was evidently not the kind of place where hysterical women stood up and punched rich white hipsters in the face. I leant over and whispered furiously in Dustin's ear. 'My fucking dad was killed in Year Zero you self-righteous prick!'

Dustin stiffened a little, moving his hands from his face. Already his eye had started to blossom pink and blue. 'Look, I'm sorry Lorn,' he said, his voice calmer now, back in control. 'Lots of people died. My friends lost relatives. And I'm not trying to belittle their deaths in any way, really I'm not. But the whole Monster thing, it's a fraud Lorna. It's ridiculous, everyone's known that for years. Go online if you don't believe me – shit, even veterans are joining the movement now. I mean, you show me one shred of evidence – one shred – and I'll… ' Dustin was standing now, facing me again. And I felt bad about his eye, I really did. But seriously, he just didn't know when to shut up. *And before I could stop myself I felt the bile rising in my throat.*

'My fucking husband *is out there now, fighting Monsters to keep pathetic little men like you safe. Why don't you ask him for some evidence?'*

And with that I walked away.

Dustin didn't call after me. For once I guess he was lost for words. As I reached the bar I slammed down a crumpled twenty, Steve not looking up to meet my eye. And then I was gone, the tears stinging my eyes before I was even out of the car park.

I was halfway down the road when I stopped and pulled over, wrenching open the car door just in time to splatter the tarmac with the contents of my stomach. I stayed there for a moment once I'd finished retching, my head on the wheel, my face a mess of snot and sick and tears. And I wanted so badly to be anywhere else but there. Then I thought of my empty apartment with its lonely little bed and I didn't want to be there either. Then I thought about Dustin and Danny and I didn't know where I wanted to be anymore. Everything just seemed broken and dirty and ruined. I lifted my head and my stomach churned again.

And maybe it wouldn't all seem so bad if I just didn't feel so goddamned
Sick.

* * *

The next morning we were sick. As before, we'd dug shallow trenches to protect us from the wind, though with Jim's damn night patrol up and runnin there weren't much sleep to be had. I was lyin in the dirt with my eyes open when I heard it. At first I thought it was an animal of some sort, this low, guttural groan that echoed around the clearin. There was a pause and then the noise came again, louder this time, more desperate. If it was an animal, then it sounded badly injured. I sat up to investigate. That's when I felt it. A hot, sharp pain in my belly, radiatin all the way through to my back. I don't know if anyone's ever stuck a knife in ya before son, but that's exactly what it felt like – as if I was bein stabbed over and over again with a long, serrated blade. As if someone were tryna finish me off. Clutchin my stomach, I attempted to get to my feet, but the ground beneath me began to tilt and my vision swam. I puked, or rather I erupted – a cascade of thin grey liquid splatterin the front of my uniform and boots as I doubled over, retchin. It stank like something dead. Through the haze of pain and stench, I gradually became aware of the animal sound again, closer this time, more urgent. I tried to look around, vaguely worried I was about to be attacked, before I finally realised the sound was coming from me. I was the animal. I puked again. Then I collapsed.

I'm not sure how long I lay there, face down in my own putrid juices, but when I opened my eyes again the sun was high in the sky and the vomit had started to form a skin. I brushed away the swarm of flies that had settled on my face and tried again to climb outta my hole. This time I succeeded, slitherin out onto a mound of sand then rollin over onto my back, gaspin to catch my breath. High above me a flock of wild geese cut across the sky, locked in a perfect V formation. I've always wondered how they do it, the geese. How they keep so organised, disciplined. Like an army when you think about it. They even got the goose step ha. I watched the birds until they disappeared, then rolled back over, this time managin to make it to my feet. Very slowly I started to make my way back towards the lake, lookin for any sign of life. It didn't take long before I found someone.

'That you Jett?' I said, croakin at the lifeless figure lying over by the ashes of the fire. The figure twitched and turned its head towards me. It was Jett alright. 'Dude I'm sick… ' he groaned. 'I think I shit my pants.' Instinctively I stuck my hand in my own boxers, relieved to find I was clean. 'Must be those fuckin berries,' I muttered as I made my way over to him. 'Trust Doggie to poison us all. You seen that fat retard anywhere? Or anyone else?' Jett shook his head, then turned green as he let rip a loud, wet-soundin fart. 'Oh Jesus… '

It was another half hour before I found Cal, huddled on the far side of the lake. He was pale and sweatin, but otherwise didn't look too bad. 'I was gonna try and clean myself up,' he said, pointin towards his sick crusted top. 'But the water don't seem too good this mornin.' I looked and saw he was right. An oily film of scum seemed to have formed on the surface of the lake overnight, thick and black and toxic. 'Don't worry about it,' I said to Cal as I helped him to his feet. 'Just wait 'till you see Jett.'

By the time we got back to the fire I was feelin much better. I was still shaky but the nausea had more or less disappeared. Jett too looked a little better, though he weren't smellin too hot, even with his trousers stripped off and a blanket tied around his waist. Now that my head was clearer I could see it weren't jus' the water that looked different in the daylight. To tell the truth, the whole place looked as sick and tired as the three of us. The palm trees that hung over us, so exotic last night, now looked frail and rotten, while even the flies that buzzed around us seemed feeble and sluggish.

Paradise it weren't.

As I kicked at the charred set of bones that lay scattered in the ashes of the fire, I heard a noise and saw what looked like a dyin cow stumblin towards us. The cow got closer, and I saw now that it was wavin at us, shoutin and tryin to get our attention. Then I saw the cow was Doggie. 'Hell… I frown gin… I frown gin!' he was yellin over and over. I turned to Cal and shrugged. 'What's the fuck's a frown gin when it's at home?' Before Cal could answer though, Doggie made another sound, one we all recognised this time. He'd stopped to throw up. 'Well at least that bastard's sick too,' spat Jett. We all nodded in agreement.

Doggie was still chuckin up when we reached him. Up close I could see jus' how bad he was, his hair drenched with sweat, his skin so pale you could almost see his teeth through the sides of his cheeks. Greedy fucker'd probably had a whole handful of berries to himself. Lookin down I noticed the puddle of vomit at his feet was streaked red. I almost felt sorry for the dumb fuck. 'I frown gin… ' he gasped again between heaves, his voice thick with bile. I glanced at Jett and Cal to see if they had any ideas. Neither of them said anythin, so I knelt down beside Doggie and slapped him as hard as I could across the face. He coughed a couple of times and turned to me, his eyes driftin into focus. 'I found Jim… '

It took another twenty minutes of slappin to get any more sense out of Doggie, and even then he only came round enough to mumble a few garbled directions before he slumped forward and passed out again. Me and Jett set off, leavin Cal to babysit. 'Don't forget to check his airways every coupla minutes,' I called back as we reached the edge of the clearin. 'And don't be scared to give him a slap if he looks like he's stopped breathin.' I might've hated the fat fuck for the berries, but I didn't want to see him dead. Not jus' yet anyway ha.

We moved as quickly as we could, which to be honest between the sickness and the blanket wrapped around Jett's legs, wasn't too fast. I was startin to feel rough again, a cold sweat pricklin my back as the sun raced towards the centre of the sky. Jett though was lookin better by the second. In fact, now that the colour had returned to his cheeks he was positively glowin. Yup, with his tangled blond hair and his eyes hidden behind an obnoxious pair of sunglasses he'd dug out from somewhere, he could probably've passed for some homo Z-list celebrity or somethin. The bastard.

After about five minutes or so Jett started to pull ahead of me, the blanket trailin behind him as his long, athletic legs propelled him forward. 'Hey, there cowboy,' I called after him. 'You'd better slow down. Don't wanta be shittin yourself all over again.' Undeterred, Jett seemed to take this as an invitation to start up a conversation. 'Hey Danny,' he said as I caught up with him. 'Did you mean all that stuff you were sayin last night? About there being no Monsters out here?' I looked over at him, his big, dumb eyes wide with expectation. What the hell was I supposed to say?

'You ever hear of a guy called Pascal?' I asked. Jett shrugged. 'Was he a footballer?' 'Close. He was a gambler. At least, he liked to bet. He was a Frog I think. Anyway, he came up with this theory that was supposed to stop kids complainin about draggin their asses outta bed to go to church each Sunday mornin. His thinkin went somethin like this. If God exists and you worship him – well good for you. You're ridin them pearly escalators all the way to heaven. If God don't exist but you pray to Him anyway, well where's the harm there? You ain't gonna know no better anyhow. Same if God don't exist and you don't believe in him. So far so good, huh? But what about if God does exist and you don't believe? What then? Well kid, as the French like to say, then you're well and truly fucked.'

Jett was silent for a while as he tried to digest this. Sure, ol' Jett's cheekbones mighta been razor sharp, but when it came to the big words he was dull as dog shit. Eventually a light came on somewhere behind those sunglasses and he nodded slowly. 'So… Pascal was sayin that a gamblin man would bet on there bein a God whether or not he thinks there is one or not?' I shook my head. 'Listen, forget God. God don't matter. What Pascal was sayin is that we should bomb the fuck out of every sandy crap hole on earth regardless of whether we really believe there're any Monsters there or not.' Jett fell silent again as he chewed this over. It was a good five minutes before he spoke again. 'So hang on, I don't get it. If Pascal proved the odds were against you, how come you said to Jim you didn't believe there were any Monsters out here?' I shrugged my shoulders. 'Because Pascal's a French cocksucker and Jim don't know shit.' I paused. 'Anyway, far as I'm concerned there's only two safe bets in life. The first one's death.' 'What's the other one?' I grinned. 'The more beautiful the woman, the worse she will fuck you over in the end.' Jett laughed pretty hard at that. 'Let me guess, you got woman trouble huh Dan?' I shrugged again. 'Well I'm still breathin ain't I?'

Jim on the other hand weren't still breathin. Jett spotted him first, over by the far west perimeter, right where Doggie had said. From a distance he looked like a fallen tree stump or something, but as we drew closer we were able to make out his medals twinklin in the sun. He was lyin face up. That's when Jett started runnin. By the time I caught up, Jett had his arm in the air, desperately searchin for a pulse. I don't know why he bothered. 'He's dead! He's fucking dead!' Jett was screamin. A sense of calm washed over me. 'Of course he's dead,' I answered. 'He's fuckin blue.' It was true, Jim's face had turned a particularly sickenin colour. His mouth was hangin open too, and the way Jett was leant over him it looked like he was tryna whisper somethin to him. To be honest it wouldn't have surprised me if he had sat up and started talkin. Ol' Jim always did like to have the last word.

'I just can't believe it,' Jett sniffed, still cradin Jim's head in his lap. His voice had gone all funny, like he was tryin really hard to stop himself hicuppin. If I didn't know better I'd said he was about to start blubbin. I decided to take control of the situation. 'I suppose we'd better bury him.' Jett stared at me, confused. 'So the crows don't get him,' I explained. Jett didn't move. 'Listen, I don't know about you but I ain't carryin him. Now I say we dig a hole and drop the poor old fucker in it. Unless you've got a better idea that is?' Jett thought for a moment. Then he shook his head. We started to dig.

The sand was harder to shift than I'd expected. There seemed to be a thick layer of silt a couple of inches below the surface, as if maybe the whole area had once been underwater. After huffin and gruntin for around half an hour, we only managed a very shallow trench, barely wide enough to cover Jim's legs. Realisin we were getting nowhere, I left Jett scrapin away on his hands and knees and went to look for somethin we could use to speed things up.

A coupla minutes later I returned with my arms full of rocks. 'What are we going to do with those?' Jett asked as I dropped them at his feet. Ignorin him, I bent down and snatched Jim's tags from his neck, pocketin 'em. Then I started to pile the rocks on Jim's face, scrabblin around for more when I ran out and stackin them up until his head was totally covered. After I'd finished I stood back and dusted off my hands, admiring my work. 'Right then,' I said, turnin to Jett. 'Job done. You ready to go?'

Jett didn't move.

'Was it the berries do you think?' he said, not takin his eyes from the pile of rocks. 'Huh?' 'That killed him. You think it was the berries?' 'Of course it was the berries!' I said, slappin him on the back. 'Well, either that or the AIDS.' I laughed. 'Now c'mon ya crazy fuck. It'll be dark soon.' Jett kept starin at the rocks. 'Only there's no sick.' 'Huh?' 'There's no sick anywhere. Or shit. Nothin. I mean, I only had a couple and look at me,' he pointed down to his bare legs. 'You'd expect there to be loads, wouldn't you? If it was enough to finish him off.' 'Listen,' I said, grabbin him around the back of the neck. 'That incompetent pricklicker Doggie has gone and handed out a bunch of poisonous berries and poor Jim here was obviously too weak to take 'em. Maybe he had a massive heart attack or maybe it gave him a blood clot in his brain. Who the fuck knows? It's jus' a horrible, horrible accident.' I paused.

'Unless… '

Jett twitched. 'Unless what?' 'Nah, forget it.' 'No, really. Unless what?' I let out a long sigh. 'Christ kid, cool it. All I was gonna say, and really I'm jus' thinkin out loud here, is unless it wasn't an accident. I mean, we both know Doggie was jealous of Jim, right?' Jett scrunched up his face. 'He was?' 'Sure he was. I mean, they're the same age, coupla years apart maybe. I think they might've even signed up together. Only, how can I put this… Doggie's career ain't exactly goin places. Thing like that can cause a lot of resentment, ya know? Turn a man funny in the head. Make him bitter.' I paused. Jett was starin at the pile of rocks again. He didn't look like he was gonna cry anymore. 'Christ, what am I sayin? Of course it was an accident. Can you honestly imagine that dipshit Doggie pullin off anythin that sophisticated? Look, let's jus' get back to the others and forget it, eh? I won't say another word about it.' I held up two fingers and saluted. 'See, scout's honour. I won't say another word.'

* * *

I waited a week before I called Dustin. For the first few days I did nothing but lie in bed feeling like shit, the nausea that had started at the Tokyo Lucky Hole having followed me home, growing to the point where I could hardly lift my head off my pillow without reaching for the sick bowl. As I lay there whimpering, it occurred to me I might be seriously ill. Could I have contracted some unpronounceable tropical disease from the patrons of Save the Animals? Or perhaps all of my guilt and resentment had finally manifested itself as a rare form of untreatable cancer? Twisting the sheets and hugging my knees to my chest, I tried to tell myself I was being ridiculous, that it was food poisoning, or flu – while the whole time visualising some deadly parasite burrowing deep down inside me, feasting on my internal organs.

In my heart I knew I only had days to live.

Towards the end of the week I started to feel a little better, even managing to make it from my bed to the sofa, where I attempted to console myself with chicken noodle soup and long stretches of daytime TV. It was no good though. No matter how hard I tried to focus on the bad acting or suspect plot lines, I couldn't stop thinking about what Dustin had said. Back in the bar, I'd been so angry I couldn't think straight. Still, as I sat watching Brad woo Charlene and Max betray Clay, the seeds of doubt that had been scattered in my direction began to sprout. Was it really possible that Year Zero had been a smokescreen to steal oil from developing nations? It sounded ridiculous, like the storyline from some hack thriller

But still…

There were definitely holes in the established story. Small questions that had bugged me over the years – or would have, if I'd ever allowed myself to ask them. Like why, in one of the most surveillance-heavy countries on the planet, hadn't anybody managed to find the Monsters yet? I mean, this was a world where an unpaid credit card bill could follow you across continents and over decades, where every square centimetre of the Earth had been mapped by satellites and drones. How could anyone, or anything, stay hidden for so long? Even when they did catch one – invariably some low-level accomplice – they always seemed to bury the body at sea or in the desert, leaving a solemn faced reporter to deliver the 'good' news. But where was the proof? The evidence that Monsters were anything other than a convenient alibi?

As the hammy actors gave way to a perma-tanned quiz show presenter, I found my head beginning to swim again

– not with sickness this time, but with confusion. I didn't know what to think anymore. And so, swallowing down my reservations, I did what every under-informed twenty-first century citizen does when they need reassurance.

I turned to the internet.

It was four in the morning before I put down my laptop. I was exhausted. What shocked me most was not the theories – which ranged from assertions that the government had fudged reports and statistics all the way to JFK-style allegations of a complete and deliberate cover-up – but the sheer number of conspiracies out there. Again I found even the simplest search seemed to throw up an unbelievable number of sites dedicated to finding out the 'truth' about Monsters, with forums containing thousands of members all offering their take on frozen frames of footage, or arguing over the official time-line of events. This time however I forced myself to look. It was like disappearing down a rabbit hole, with each page linking to a hundred more, the views becoming more extreme, the 'evidence' becoming more persistent. Everybody had their own take on who was responsible and what their motivations might be, but despite the disparate views there was one claim that was repeated over and over again:

We were being lied to.

Even after I'd managed to tear myself away from the screen, I still sat there for a long time, unable, or unwilling, to sleep. Eventually the sun started to come up, grey light spilling into the apartment, illuminating the circle of used coffee mugs that surrounded me. A rumble of traffic officially signalled the start of another day, the first rattle of rat-racers clawing their way to the office, middle managers gargling petrol station espressos while cocooned in their luxury child-killing cars. And very soon the whole city would be awake, the young and the old, the rich and the poor, and everyone in between. Churning like the contents of my stomach. And across the sea villages were being flattened and collaborators were being tortured and young men and women were getting their arms and legs blown off. All to keep the wheels a'turning. The people working. The oil flowing.

Or so the story goes.

I looked at the clock, amazed to see it was almost eight, the rumble outside now risen to a roar, the light burning so bright through my open blinds that the apartment looked as though it was on fire. And right then I knew what I had to do. I picked up the phone and dialled.

I waited for Dustin to answer.

THREE

We never walk at night. That's when Monsters attack.

Or so they say.

As for me, I'm not too sure. I mean, look at Year Zero. Don't get much brighter or bluer than that. Nah, I've always found the scariest things happen in broad daylight.

Right under your nose.

Anyway, we never walked at night. That was Jim's rule. Now though Jim was dead, and the way I saw it was we weren't gonna get much more lost than we already were.

'Jesus, with our luck the dark will probably *increase* our chances of bumpin into somewhere,' I said once we'd got back and told the others about Jim. Doggie was still too ill to offer much of an opinion, but Jett and Cal agreed straight away. Seems they thought the place was cursed now, what with the berries and all. Jett explained he'd been doin some calculations, and he reckoned there was no point headin north towards the airstrip anymore. By his reckonin we must have covered hundreds of kilometres in the last few days and in all likelihood we'd probably walked straight past without noticin.

Jett picked up a stick to make his point. Sketchin roughly in the sand, he drew a big circle for the base, a tiny triangle for the airstrip and an even smaller cross for the oasis. He was right. We were nowhere near it. Then he drew a large jagged line in the sand, a sort of bolt of lightnin to the left of the triangle. 'This is the border,' he said. 'You see how close we are to it?' He was right again. The cross and the lightnin bolt *were* close. From where I was standin it looked like you could make it in one small hop. 'Now if I've figured it right, we could be at the border in less than three days. Two if we're lucky. We just need to start movin west and we should plough straight into it. Then we… '

A loud, wet cough interrupted Jett and we turned to see Doggie had stumbled over to join us. 'What… hack-hack… about… hack-hack… our orders?' I shook my head in disbelief. Doggie looked like shit, his cheeks flushed purple from coughin, his chin shiny with spit. 'Listen Dog… ' I started, but Jett leapt in. 'Orders? You want to talk about orders now, you fucking retard? What orders were you following when you decided to poison Jim? I'll give you something to cough about… ' Jett took a step towards Doggie, his fist raised. I reached out and grabbed Jett lightly by the arm. 'Ok, everybody jus' calm down. It's been a bad day. Hell, it's been a doozy. But that ain't no reason for people to start losin their heads. Now as it happens, I tend to agree with Jett here. Far as I'm concerned we should head west and head quickly. Unless anyone's got anythin to say that is?' Cal and Jett shook their heads. I turned to Doggie. 'Dog, anythin you want to add?'

Doggie eyeballed me for a coupla seconds, still doubled over. He wiped his chin with the back of his hand and then, very slowly, he shook his head. 'No,' he croaked. I took a step towards him. 'No, what?' I hissed. Doggie scrunched up his face, genuinely confused. 'Huh?' I took another step towards him, close enough so that I could lift up my boot and land it square in his nuts. If I felt like it, that is. 'No, what?' I asked again. He shook his head again, unsure of what he was supposed to say. This time I leant forward so that I was only a coupla inches from his ear. 'No, *Sir*… ' I whispered. Doggie's whole body went stiff. I waited there, so close I could smell the stink of vomit on his breath. Then all of a sudden he let out a long sigh, as if someone'd stuck a hole in his side. Even his body seemed to sag in the middle. 'No

Sir,' he mumbled. 'That's better!' I said, straightenin up and givin him a playful slap on the back. 'Right then troops, we'd better get goin if we want to make the border by breakfast!' Jett shot me a grin.

'Yes Sir!'

* * *

I don't know what I'd imagined. A couple of dozen Dustins maybe; well-dressed hipsters with a designer beer in one hand and a smartphone in the other, all of them making snarky comments to each other and live-tweeting their frustrations with the establishment. In reality though, it was more like a carnival, a sea of people from all walks of life – school children and OAPs, business men and punks, Muslims and Christians and, well, a few people who looked like Dustin – all of them stood shoulder-to-shoulder, banners held high in the air, fists clenched in solidarity, slowly shuffling forwards, marching.

Like an army.

'What is all this?' I'd asked when we arrived. Dustin shook his head. 'Jesus little miss army wife – where have you been? We do this every year!'

I'd met Dustin outside Save the Animals about an hour before the shop was due to open. We let ourselves in and sat facing each other over mugs of budget instant coffee. His eye had healed, although there was still a faint shadow underneath from where I'd hit him. I didn't mention it and neither did he. Instead we focused on the details of the protest. Dustin had a map of the city and using a biro he traced a line from the shop to the city centre, pointing out places of interest along the route – likely police barricades and gang hotspots and other places we should avoid if we didn't plan on getting our heads kicked in. 'A guy I was with last year got a brick chucked at him outside a bar,' explained Dustin. 'He was in hospital for a month. Lost a couple of teeth. They got the guy who did it, but they let him off with a fine. Turns out he was an off-duty soldier.' I thought about Danny, picturing what he'd do if he bumped into an anti-war protestor outside a bar. Secretly I thought the guy was lucky only to lose a couple of teeth.

I decided not to say anything.

Dustin ran through the rest of the route, drained his mug, then folded up the map and slipped it into his pocket. We started for the door and then he stopped, remembering something. Tearing a sheet of paper from the pad next to the till, he took the biro and quickly scribbled a couple of lines. 'Stick this on the door will you,' he said. I took the note and read:

Shop closed due to revolution.
Back at 2 :)

I don't know whether it was nerves, but by the time we reached the start of the march I was feeling sick again. People crowded all around, shoving into me, yelling, laughing, pulling me along with them, while the whole time I gripped tightly to Dustin's arm and held on for dear life. Normally I wouldn't have minded the rabble – I'd been to enough raves and rock concerts in my life to be able to deal with having someone else's armpit shoved in my face – but that day I was feeling particularly delicate. For one thing, my sense of smell seemed to have developed an almost super-human sensitivity; the mixture of tobacco smoke, chip fat, exhaust fumes and body odour melding together to form a sickening fug, so thick I felt I could almost see it. I swallowed hard, willing myself not to vomit. I turned to Dustin. 'You know if I'm going to do this I might have to get a little bit high first.' Dustin looked at me and nodded seriously.

'That can be arranged.'

Half an hour later I was shuffling forward with the rest of the herd. The nausea was still present, but it no longer bothered me so much, a thin protective bubble having formed around me. I hadn't smoked weed since my last year at school, and even though Dustin had only managed to score a tiny amount it was enough to leave me feeling happily disconnected – which considering the personal hygiene of some of my fellow protestors was no bad thing.

As we bobbed towards the town square, I found myself focusing on small details around me. It was particularly interesting to watch the people standing on the sidelines of the march; the school children playing truant on their bikes, the businessmen barking into their mobile phones as they waited to cross the street, the shopkeepers standing outside their empty stores and cafes. For the most part they looked indifferent, even faintly amused. We were a freak show, a circus come to town – a ragtag assortment of the mad, the bad and the seriously deluded. And yet we outnumbered the onlookers ten-to-one. Maybe even twenty-to-one. Surely that had to mean something?

'Shit, look out!'

Dustin grabbed my arm and pulled me out of the path of a giant police horse. I reached out as it passed, patting its muscular haunch. 'Careful,' Dustin said. 'I got bit by one of those fuckers last year… Although to be fair I was trying to feed it a space cake.' I laughed as we edged away, the policeman in the saddle twirling his baton menacingly. There was a squeal of feedback as someone turned on a megaphone, and then the chanting started:

Not-in-my-name!

Out-out-troops-get-out!

And a million other blasphemous lines I'd never heard before. I looked around at the people yelling, hands in the air like football hooligans or eyes closed like church-goers, men, women and children all belting out every syllable, not dropping a beat. And I thought: they're mad. All of them. Completely mad. Yet it was a madness I recognised – it was the same look I'd seen on the faces of the young soldiers at Danny's passing out parade. Only where there had been cold hatred in the soldiers' eyes, the protestors all stared blissfully skywards, glowing with a collective confidence that they were in the right, that they could make a difference, just by being here, together. That not another drop of blood would be spilt. That not another life would be lost.

At least

Not-in-my-naaaaaame!!

The crowd began to surge as we neared the city centre, the chanting growing more intense, the stink rising as people tumbled into one another while the police stood impotently aside, outnumbered, outgunned; a hundred-to-one now. And still the people swarmed, sucking up all of the available oxygen from the atmosphere, exhaling only love and righteousness in return. And for a second I thought I was going to faint. And then a teenage boy barged into me and nearly toppled me over and I grabbed onto Dustin's arm for support and he turned to me and yelled: 'Isn't this great?' And I started laughing because I realised it was *great. And then another joint appeared from nowhere, passed over the heads of the strangers. And I took a hit and passed it on. And the sun was shining, breaking through the clouds. And there were a million of us now, a billion. Hands in the air. Screaming. And then someone handed me a banner and I let go of Dustin and raised it up high in the air. And I started to chant along with everyone else:*

Out, out, out.

And together we sounded like one voice.

And we were going to win.

* * *

It took us about an hour to pack up. We decided to dump anythin heavy, leavin most of our spare clothes and beddin behind to make space for the flasks and bottles we'd filled with the gritty, black water from the oasis. Naturally, we kept hold of our guns too. Monsters or not, there were things out there you'd rather not meet unarmed. I'd heard the wogs can be particularly hostile out west. Local militias, gangs of rebels armed to the teeth – the fuckin Wild West, we called it. Landmines, tank busters – I even heard of 'em strappin bombs to animals. Can ya imagine that! Baa-Baa-BOOM! Ha. It sounds like the bad ol' days all over again. Back before we killed everyone. Anyway, I weren't plannin on takin any chances. I have a rule out here, son: *If it don't look like you – shoot it.* Sure, it might not be politically correct and whatnot, but it's worked for me so far. *Shoot it, and keep shootin until you're sure that it's dead.*

We were almost done packin when Cal appeared and called me to one side. Seems he had some stuff he needed to get off his chest. 'Excuse me Sir, um… Permission to speak freely?' I nodded. 'Well no offence, Dan… Sir, but I don't know how else to say this. I think I'm losin my mind.' I looked at him and laughed. I had to admit, the kid didn't look too hot. Unlike Jett, Cal didn't tan. His face was a red mess of blisters, and he had dark circles around his eyes. 'I ain't been feelin too good, Sir,' he continued. 'Not good at all. And it's not jus' the berries. It's my head. I jus' keep thinkin about poor ol' Jim out on the post, all alone. And then there're all the others and… I don't want to die out here, Sir. I got my little sister at home, and you know my mum ain't been too well. I don't know how she'd take it. And… and… ' Cal trailed off, his eyes startin to water.

'That's enough, soldier!' I barked. 'If there's one thing I can't stand it's self-pity. I know we're in a tight spot, but we'll get through it. We've got a new plan, remember? Three days and we'll be at the border.' Cal rubbed his eyes, tryin to hold his shit together. 'I know that, Sir. It's jus' everytime I think about walkin again I… Christ, I don't even know if I can bring myself to pick up my pack,' he pointed down at his faded rucksack, bottles of cloudy grey water spillin out the top of it. Suddenly I had an idea. 'Hey Dog!' I yelled. 'Get over here!'

Sure enough a coupla minutes later Doggie staggered into view, his own pack strapped to his back. He was still fuckin green. 'Now listen Dog,' I said as he reached us. 'Cal here ain't feelin too hot and we agreed that it'd probably be for the best if you carried his bag for him. Least for the first day.' Doggie stared at me, tryna work out if I was messin with him or not. When he saw that I wasn't he started to protest. 'Hey listen Dan, I'm still not feelin too great myself. Plus I've got this on my back already. Where'd ya want me to stick it?' I shot Doggie a great big smile.

One of the keys to being an effective leader is empathy. It's important you put yourself into your subordinates' shoes, see things from their perspective and whatnot.

Well son, I got empathy by the bucketload.

I grabbed Doggie by his fat neck and punched him square in the jaw. 'IT'S SIR YOU IGNORANT COCKSUCKIN MOTHERFUCKER AND THIS AIN'T A CONVERSATION. I DON'T CARE IF YOU STICK IT UP YOUR FLABBY FAGGOT ASS! NOW UNLESS YOU WANT TO END UP LIKE YOUR FUCKIN CAT YOU BETTER CARRY IT, DO YOU UNDERSTAND?' Doggie picked himself up off the floor, nodded once and stumbled off, draggin Cal's bag behind him.

I turned back to Cal and smiled. 'There now, all sorted. Are you ready?'

We walked for two days straight. I mean it. All night we marched, with only the stars and the faint glow of our torches to guide us, the sand like compacted ice under our boots. Then when the sun came up behind us in the mornin we switched off our flashlights, stripped down to our vests and kept goin. We stuck close together this time, Jett, Cal and me walkin shoulder to shoulder, with Doggie a coupla steps ahead so we could keep an eye on him. Every so often he would slow down or complain that the straps on Cal's bag were cutting into him and Jett would have to give him a dig with the butt of his rifle. Apart from that we moved in silence, mainly because there was nothing to say. The hunger was bad, ten times worse than before we stopped. I guess it was all the pukin or somethin. We were properly empty now, save for the dirty water we swigged near enough constantly from our flasks in the desperate hope it'd fill us up. Whenever my teeth weren't chatterin I could hear it swishin in my belly. It made me think of the sea.

Occasionally someone would need the toilet and we would stop and wait while they took a piss or squatted down and took a liquid shit in the sand, not botherin to dig a hole or even wipe before they pulled up their pants. Then we would carry on. Coupla times Dog said he needed to stop. We kept goin, letting him soil himself. Figured he stank so bad it wouldn't make a difference anyhow, ha.

After the second night we were dead on our feet. Seriously, we might as well've been walkin backwards. Eventually, I gave the order to stop. 'Ok, that's it boys. We're takin a break,' I said, pointin to a large boulder near to where we'd stopped. 'We can sleep in the shade. Jus' four hours, then we'll get movin again.'

Cal and Doggie gave a quiet groan of relief as they dropped to their knees and started wrestlin with their bags. Jett though, remained standin. 'Woah, now hang on there. With all due respect Sir, do you think it's wise to leave no one standin guard?' he said, shootin me a wicked grin. 'An excellent point, soldier,' I grinned back. 'But who would act so selflessly in the interest of the team? Anyone?'

Nobody said anythin.

'Anyone?' I asked again. Doggie looked at his feet. 'Ah, Private Doggerel. Good of ya to volunteer. Your country loves you. Now get to your post. Come wake us in four hours.' Doggie stared at me, his big dopey cow eyes fillin with water. He started to say somethin, but Jett took a step towards him and he shut his mouth. 'Thanks Dog!' I yelled as he trudged off to keep watch. Then I bedded down under the rock with the others.

When I woke it was dark. I shook the others and crawled out from under the boulder. I couldn't believe it. Fuckin Doggie had let us oversleep. I swore to God when I got hold of him I was gonna whip his ass good.

Only I never did get hold of him.

We called and called but there was no answer. Jett even went off huntin for him with a flashlight, but there was no sign of him. Then Cal noticed Doggie's bag had gone. 'Well that's that,' I said. 'Damn coward's run out on us.'

But that wasn't that. Because a little later, when I went in my bag to fetch a drink I found my flask had gone. I asked Cal for a sip of his, but that had gone too. So had Jett's. Doggie had left us. And he'd taken the water with him.

* * *

I sat in the waiting room downing plastic cups of mineral water. I must have got up to refill my cup thirty times in the half hour I'd been sat there, the loud rumble of the water cooler echoing around the walls as I crouched in front of the machine, studiously avoiding the eyes of the other patients until finally – finally *– I felt the need to pee and rushed to the bathroom to fill my little test tube. After that it was just a matter of sitting there until my name was called, pretending to read twenty-year-old copies of* Homemaker Magazine *while I waited to be diagnosed with stomach cancer. Or ebola. Or any of the other ugly, painful and ultimately fatal diseases that matched my current symptoms – namely the need to throw up every couple of hours, along with a generalised feeling of impending doom.*

Basically it was business as usual, only with added vomit.

As I sat there, I found myself thinking back to the rally the day before. I'd been exhausted by the time the march had finally finished – ready to crawl into bed and hibernate for a week. Dustin had other ideas though. It had taken over an hour for the crowds to disperse from the central square, leaving behind them a thick blanket of litter; beer cans, cigarette butts, wrappers, discarded flags and placards. Once enough people had filtered away I started to head in the direction we'd come from, back towards the shop. Dustin caught my sleeve though, tugging me back towards him. 'Why don't you come for a drink? I'm meeting some people later.' I thought back to the last time I'd seen Dustin drunk. 'You know, I'm still not feeling too great. I think I've picked up a stomach bug and... ' Dustin started shaking his head 'Oh come off it! Didn't you have fun this afternoon?' I gave a small, sleepy shrug. 'Sure.' 'Exactly! Just like I promised,' Dustin said, already beginning to pull me in the opposite direction. 'Listen, the bar we're meeting at is just down the road. If you don't like it then you can leave, no problem.' Dustin kept pulling me as he spoke, the rubbish crunching under my feet like fresh snow, or dead leaves. 'But you will like it. These people, they're not like the people who came out today. They were just here to party – to get drunk and high and feel good about themselves for a couple of hours before they go back to their boring little lives. They don't really believe *they can change anything. But the people I'm going to meet now... ' Dustin grinned again. 'Listen you'll have fun, I promise.'*

The bar Dustin led me to was called The Hobgoblin. Although it stood wedged between a row of ultra-trendy Thai restaurants and recently refurbished wine bars, it was a stubbornly traditional pub – a hand painted sign of a demon swinging above the doorway and thick coils of ivy clinging to the crumbling brickwork. Apart from a small glow of light visible through the smeared front window, it looked almost entirely derelict. Inside was no different, and as I followed Dustin through the door I was greeted by a handful of empty wooden stools propped against a deserted bar. Dustin didn't look phased however, and as I followed him to a small doorway on the other side of the room I had the impression he'd visited this place many times before.

The doorway led to a narrow set of stairs, the exposed

brickwork curving steeply downwards, the darkness lit only by a couple of flickering candles – actual candles *– long streaks of red wax forming thick stalactites below the rusted holders. 'Jeremy has a real sense of theatre,' Dustin said by way of explanation as we descended the stairs together, me clinging tightly to the back of his shirt, terrified I was about to fall and break my leg. I found myself vaguely wondering if I was being led to some sort of medieval sex dungeon.*

At the bottom of the stairs the room opened up into a large basement with a low wooden ceiling, again lit only by candles. At the back of the room was a group of four suited men huddled around a small table, heads bowed conspiratorially. As I followed Dustin through the gloom the men turned around, revealing a silver laptop open on the table between them, looking strangely futuristic amongst the rustic brick and wood.

'Ah, Dusty!' said the man closest to us, his strange accent hovering somewhere between South London and South Africa.

'Jeremy!' Dustin said, rushing forward and pumping the man's hand. 'Great to see you again!'

Moving closer, I was able to make out Jeremy's features in the candlelight, a mop of translucent white-blonde hair falling over his pale face. He looked like he hadn't seen daylight for a few months. Even more interesting though was the screen flashing next to him.

From where I was standing I could make out grainy video footage of what looked like a school bus travelling along a rocky desert road. The camera pulled back, half a kilometre, two kilometres, and I realised why the image was so shaky. It was being shot from inside the cockpit of a helicopter. Suddenly there was a burst of light as a missile fizzed to life at the bottom of the screen, the camera tracking it until it made contact with its target – the bus. A huge fireball filled the screen then froze, looking like some sort of weird flower, its ragged petals blooming orange, red, yellow, black. Jeremy had paused the film.

I glanced up to find a strange look stretched across his sallow face. 'And this must be... ?' he asked, not taking his eyes from me. Dustin coughed awkwardly. 'Um yes, sorry. Jeremy this is Lorna. Lorna – Jeremy.' Jeremy kept staring at me for a couple more seconds, his eyes searching me, boring little holes into my skin. Then he blinked and his face cracked into a broad grin. 'Good to have you here Lorna. Any friend of Dusty's is a friend of the cause.' I waved awkwardly, my eyes flicking involuntarily back to the screen where the explosion was still frozen. 'Ah, so you're enjoying our little home video eh?' Jeremy said, following my gaze. 'We've got hours of this stuff. Terabytes of it. But enough,' he paused, bringing down the lid of the computer. 'Come take a seat. Have a drink. We have lots to talk about.'

The conversation seemed to go on for hours, moving in endless, impenetrable circles. At first I tried to keep up, nodding or shaking my head whenever it seemed appropriate, but I quickly lost the thread altogether, letting the talk of secret surveillance and 'incontrovertible evidence' wash over me while I sat and studied the men as they talked. Everyone seemed desperate to impress Jeremy I noticed, looking to him for approval whenever they spoke while he sat at the head of the table, his fingers pressed together, a carefully crafted look of concern on his face. I don't know why, but I found him almost unbearably irritating. Who did this man think he was? Sat down here in his ridiculous candlelit cavern with his co-conspirators, like bloody Guy Fawkes. It was all just so irretrievably... naff. And yet the others couldn't get enough of it. Dustin in particular seemed ridiculously excited, his face screwed into a passionate scowl, banging the table with his fist as he spoke. I wondered if all revolutionaries started out like this? Lenin, Mao Tse-Tung, Che Guevara. Little boys, playing the part they thought the world expected of them.

As I sat there growing more and more resentful that I'd let Dustin drag me here under the pretence of 'fun', I gradually became aware that the others kept turning round to glance at me. Shuffling uncomfortably in my seat, I forced myself to tune in to the conversation, paranoid they were talking about me. Suddenly Jeremy clapped his hands together for silence. 'Enough! But we are forgetting our manners. We have a guest with us – and a soldier's wife no less... ' I turned to stare at Dustin, who was refusing to look up, apparently fascinated by a spot on the table. Jeremy continued, turning to talk to me directly. 'My apologies Lorna. Now if you can spare us a few more minutes I'd like to show you another video? I think you'll find this one particularly... enlightening.' Before I could say anything, Jeremy had re-opened the laptop and loaded the file he was looking for.

He hit play.

The footage was even shakier than in the first video, looking like it might have been shot from the back of a truck, the camera jumping up and down as it tracked across a featureless stretch of sand. After thirty seconds or so the image seemed to settle down as the lorry slowed to a stop and whoever was filming stood up and started walking slowly towards a rubbish dump. There was scratchy confusion while the camera strained to focus. And then I saw it.

What had looked from a distance like rubbish was in fact the littered corpses of thirty or forty men, gaping bullet wounds in the back of their heads, their hair and beards slick with blood. The cameraman continued to move forward through the field of bodies, stopping occasionally to zoom in on a particularly deep wound, or a vivid facial expression, one man's mouth twisted into a stiff blue scream. To the edge of the frame the soldiers – for it was obvious now that that was what they were – could be seen bending down to check the bodies, picking them up by their hair and letting them slump back to the floor.

This went on for another minute or so, before the scene abruptly cut and then restarted with a close up of two soldiers. There was no sound on the video and the two men were opening and closing their mouths as if they were drowning, tears rolling down their faces.

I realised they were laughing.

The camera panned back slowly to reveal what was so funny. One of the men was holding a corpse by the hair. The corpse was a boy. The camera zoomed in again to focus on the large open wound on the back of the boy's head.

Then I saw what was so funny.

One of the soldiers, the one holding the dead boy, had his trousers bunched around his knees. I watched as he forced his erect penis into the wound, the camera following as he danced.

In out.

In out.

While the soldiers stood around laughing.

In total silence.

Jeremy paused the video. 'I think we all get the idea?' he said, closing the lid of the laptop again. 'And we have hours of this stuff. Weeks of it. Of course, you can imagine what would happen if this was to end up in the wrong – or should that be right – hands… ' He paused, twisting to stare directly at me. 'What about you Lorna? Do you think the world deserves to see this stuff? Do you think people have a right to know what's really going on?'

I looked at him, a Tube map of purple veins visible under that paper white complexion, his forehead clammy with perspiration. I glanced over at Dustin, who had gone almost as pale as Jeremy, and then I opened my mouth.

And vomited straight onto the table.

I made an appointment at the doctors the very next morning.

'Well Lorna, the good news is we've managed to rule out anything nasty. Your blood sugars are fine… '

I looked up at the doctor, stunned not to be hearing the death sentence I'd expected.

'… In fact, as it is I can't see there's anything wrong, apart from perhaps a touch of anaemia… '

I shook my head, confused. It didn't make sense. The vomiting, the stomach cramps – couldn't this woman see I was dying?

'... And the morning sickness of course. Some women do seem to get it rather bad I'm afraid, but hopefully it should start to level out soon. Do you know how far along you are?'

* * *

It's incredible when you think about how much punishment the human body can take. I mean, people say the average human male needs 2500 thousand calories a day just to maintain a constant weight, so for a soldier you can triple that. Now in the last week all I've eaten besides a coupla dozen sandflies is a few mouthfuls of burnt cat meat and two or three poisoned berries, yet besides a bit of bellyache and bad breath I've hardly noticed the hunger. A few hours without water though, and I'd begun to shut down. My lips were raw and cracked, my tongue swollen in my head. This time I didn't even bother suckin on stone. I knew the drill by now. I just had to keep walkin.

As the scenery cycled through white, brown, grey and beige, I realised with certainty that I was going to die out here. Even if we came across another oasis, hell, even if we managed to find the border, we would only be postponing the inevitable. Sooner or later, we would stop and we would fall. The birds would strip us of our meat and the sun would bleach our bones and eventually we would disappear as if we had never been; earth-to-earth, ashes-to-ashes, dust-to-dust. Sand-to-sand ha. And the strange thing was, this time I didn't particularly care.

As the three of us bobbed along in silence, even Jett seemin to have finally run out of steam, I found myself struck by the idea I was unravelling – as if a little piece of me had become snagged somewhere, at the oasis or back at the camp, or even further away maybe, an invisible thread stretchin out over the ocean, all the way back home to you. Either way, I couldn't escape the feelin I was slowly being pulled apart, that with each step forward there was somehow a little less of me left to go on, that sooner or later I would simply disappear.

On top of this, I'd started seein things again. At first it was just random images – fragments, with no context or explanation. A cloud that reminded me of an old hat I used to wear, a rock that sorta resembled a dentist's chair. Gradually though, the pictures began to fall into an order I could follow, the scenery givin way to a full-blown slideshow. My life, tricklin before my eyes. There I was as a baby, bonnie and full of life, exactly as I was in the framed photo on Mum's dressin table, head-to-toe in scratchy home-knit, frozen mid-smile – wind she always joked – and there I was again, a six-year-old starin at that same picture through a crack in Mum's closet, hidin from a hidin ha. The pictures accelerated, the years fluttered past: my first day at school, the first guy I knocked out, my first blowjob – all of the major milestones basically, until finally I reached your mother. Then time stopped.

Lorna.

Yup, that's one thing I'll say about your mum – of all the mistakes I've made, she's definitely my favourite.

My private show-reel was interrupted by a loud scrapin noise, as if the projector had packed up. I blinked and I was back in the desert. The scrapin noise again. It was Cal. He was tryin to say somethin. He looked excited. 'We… made… it… !' I followed his finger to where he was pointin and saw a thin black line stretchin across the horizon, slicin the sand in two. It was a fence. We had reached the border. It was my turn to make a noise.

Twenty minutes later the three of us stood on the other side. The fence, although made of razor wire, was only a metre or so high and we all managed to clear it in a single hop. Fuck knows who they were expectin to keep out. Midgets? Ha. Cal was the last to jump, and once he made it across, the three of us hopped around like fuckin idiots for a bit, high-fivin and gettin each other in headlocks and shit. Jett looked so happy I thought he was gonna blub. Shit, even I felt a bit choked.

After we finished celebratin we stood there for a coupla minutes and looked around. It was weird. For some reason I'd always figured things would look different on the other side of the border. But nah. The sun was still just as hot. The sand was just as brown and gritty. The horizon was still full of nothing but sky. Most of all I was still dying of thirst. I could tell by the others' faces they were all thinkin the same thing. Cal was the first to speak. 'So what now?' I turned to Jett. 'Yeah. So what now?' Jett did a little squinty thing with his eyes, peerin off into the distance. He looked left, right, behind him, then bent down and picked up a handful of sand. I waited for him to pop a finger in his mouth and stick it in the wind. 'So what now?' I said again. Jett stood up. 'Well… I guess we keep walking.' I turned to Cal and nodded. 'Yup,' I said. Cal agreed. 'Yup.' And we started walkin.

I don't know how far we'd walked. It was almost dusk, the light that sickly yellow it sometimes goes before a thunderstorm. There weren't a cloud in the sky though. There weren't nothin nowhere. We'd spread out again, Jett up front, me in the middle and Cal at the back. Cal. I had to admit I felt sorry for the kid. No one tells ya about this shit when you're joinin up. Nah. Ya think you're gonna be battlin Monsters with a machine gun or tossin grenades out the back of a helicopter. I wondered if Cal'd fired a gun since basic. I wondered if he'd ever killed anyone. Every time I glanced back over my shoulder he seemed a little smaller, as if he was shrinkin in the heat. Fadin away. I half wondered if I shouldn't put him out of his misery. One quick pop in the back of the head and it'd all be over. The pain. The hunger. The thirst. He wouldn't feel a thing. I mean, you'd do it for a dog. Or a cat for that matter ha.

Jus' then Jett gave a cry from the front. I raced to catch up with him, prayin to God he had somethin better to show me than a battered metal sign and a roll of chicken wire. When

I got there Jett had dropped his pack on the floor and was stood perfectly still with his eyes closed. My first guess was sunstroke.

'Okay soldier,' I croaked as I stepped closer to him. 'We all get it. You're overheated is all. We'll take a rest for a few minutes and… ' Jett shook his head violently. 'Shhhh!' I smiled as nicely as I could. Poor kid was fuckin cooked. Instinctively I felt my hand move towards my gun. Maybe it would be for the best? Do them both and then myself. Right then and there. It was either that or wait till we all ended up as batshit crazy as Jett.

'Listen!' Jett said. 'There it is again. Can you hear it?' I smiled, my finger closin round the trigger. 'I hear it, soldier. I hear… ' I stopped. I really could hear somethin, a light, tinklin sound, like broken glass on the breeze.

'Hey guys?' Cal had finally caught up. 'I think I need to get sick… ' 'Shhhh!' I hissed at him. 'Listen.' We all stood and listened. The noise was definitely there, faint but gettin louder every second, high and familiar, almost exactly like a… bell. 'Look!' shouted Jett. We all watched in silence as a small white dot appeared on the horizon and started movin towards us. As the dot got bigger the sound got louder, until it was close enough for us to see that it *was* a bell. It was a bell tied around the neck of a goat. I shook my head, wonderin if the other two were seein what I was seein. 'Now where in hell do you suppose…? ' I started, but before I could finish Jett was crouched down and movin towards it, his rifle already drawn. 'Come on,' he whispered over his shoulder. 'Dinner time!'

Even though the goat was still a fair way off, it'd obviously caught our scent and as we moved closer it froze, lowerin its head uncertainly. 'Shit! It's seen us. I don't want to risk scaring it off,' Jett said, lowerin his gun and dartin off to the left. 'Should I go after him Sir?' Cal asked.

I hesitated.

Somethin about the animal didn't seem right. I mean,

I'd heard of wild goats before, but this one had a bell round its neck. Which meant somebody had to have put it there. But who? I took a couple of steps closer. Somehow Jett had already managed to get right behind the animal and was slowly creepin up on it, his rifle drawn, lookin for a clear shot. 'Should I go after him Sir?' Cal asked again. I cupped my hands to my eyes. The goat seemed to have some sort of saddle too, somethin black and bulky tied to its back. I took another coupla steps closer. And that's when I realised. 'Oh shi… ' I started to say, but never got to finish.

Oh shi…

* * *

Shit.

Shit, shit, shit.

I was on my way to meet Dustin, the sun stuttering through gaps in the bloated grey sky, like something good determined to push through the gloom. I rapped the steering wheel as I drove, trying to stay upbeat. Dustin had called the previous evening to tell me about a last minute protest that was being staged outside an air-base and I'd jumped at the chance to go – if only to distract myself from the circular thoughts that had been swilling around my skull since my trip to the doctors. The main one being:

How the fuck can I be pregnant?

There had only been that one time, the night Danny left. It didn't make sense.

Except of course it did make sense. The tiredness, nausea, stomach cramps – not to mention the fact I'd skipped my last three periods. In fact it seemed impossible I'd not known immediately. I thought back to my first biology lessons a million years ago, a crumpled textbook with a cartoon strip of Mr Sperm and Mrs Egg.

How do you do and how do you do and how do you do again?

Of course I'd known. I'd known all along. I just didn't want to believe it was true. So instead I'd told myself I was run down, stressed out, overworked, while deep inside me a secret was growing. A secret that was now exactly fifteen weeks old and, at least according to the internet, about the size of an apple.

That secret was you.

But I didn't want to think about any of that right then – couldn't think about it. Not when there was so much else that needed to happen first. Since I'd watched Jeremy's video I'd become convinced that what Dustin was doing was right. Whether or not there really were Monsters out there (and neither Dustin nor Jeremy had shown me any evidence that there weren't) there was no denying people were being butchered in my name. In my dad's name. I owed it to him to raise my voice above the TV and the radio and the newspapers and shout 'No!'

Even if nobody listened.

Obviously I hadn't had a chance to talk to Danny yet, and I knew it was going to be difficult for him to accept. But who knew – maybe he'd have seen things over there that had changed his mind? After all, Dustin had talked about veterans joining the movement. Either way, I'd finally found a place in the world I could make a difference, and not even the shock of finding out I was fifteen weeks pregnant was going to stop me.

By the time I met Dustin the sun had burnt off nearly all the cloud, the temperature soaring so that as we trekked together to the meeting spot – yet another bar – I felt the tops of my arms starting to burn. Draping my shirt over my shoulders I turned to Dustin, noticing his worried expression. 'So how many people are we expecting today? A thousand? More?' I asked, forcing myself to stay focused on the task in hand. The medicine the doctor had prescribed had helped with the nausea but not the tiredness – not that I'd been able to get much sleep over the last week with everything that had gone on. Instead I'd stayed up until the early hours reading about the changes that my body was undergoing, looking in the mirror to see if I could spot the first signs of a tell-tale bump. Anything to make it seem real. 'Er, probably a few less than that,' Dustin mumbled, mopping his face with the edge of his t-shirt. 'But for once I don't think size is important. In fact in some ways it might be better if there's less of us. What with the security issues… ' I nodded, not really listening. Maybe I should just come out with it? Dustin, I'm pregnant. *I'd cry for a couple of minutes then he'd make a bitchy joke and that would be that. Business as usual. Only I wouldn't feel so terribly alone. I'd made up my mind, ready to speak. And then*

'Ah, we're here!'

I looked up, confused. Ahead was a small, wooden shack standing alone in a field – more of a shed than a pub. Above the door was a scruffy, hand painted sign that read: The Bumpkin. *At the splintering wooden table out the front sat six or seven men and women who stood up to greet us. I was confused. Unlike Dustin or Jeremy, these people seemed to belong to another time, as if they had recently been dug out of a nineties time capsule. Two of the women had dreadlocks and at least three of them were wearing tie-dye. One of the men had his top off, and appeared to have a large CND symbol tattooed on his shoulder, right below a smudged dolphin jumping over a rainbow. I glanced down at my own plain t-shirt and jeans, feeling for perhaps the first time in my adult life completely overdressed for the occasion.*

Declining several kind offers of a can of Special Brew, I took my place with Dustin around the table, desperately trying to catch his eye to gauge whether this was all part of some elaborate joke. A large technical drawing was spread in the centre, blue lines and grids criss-crossing the paper. Despite not having Jeremy's fashion sense, these people nevertheless shared his enthusiasm for a good prop. 'Just over this hill is an airbase,' Dustin whispered, gesturing to a steep incline behind The Bumpkin. 'The bastards are flying new recruits out on a weekly basis, shipping walking corpses to the front line from right under our noses. A couple of weeks ago Jeremy managed to get a copy of the blueprints for their generator so now we're planning on paying them a little visit.' As he said this a short, fat woman with green hair turned to me and grinned, reaching into her bag to show off a pair of wire cutters. 'Should slow 'em down a bit, huh?' she wheezed. I smiled politely.

We're doomed, I thought. Doomed.

Getting into the base was surprisingly easy; it had taken maybe twenty minutes in total, including the long walk up to the unguarded security fence. 'For once I guess we should be thankful for budget cuts. This should be easy,' Dustin hissed, as the fat girl – who I'd found out was actually called Mossy – set to work with the wire cutters. Glancing up at a small yellow sign hanging from the fence I wasn't so sure I agreed:

All trespassers will be shot on sight

Somewhere deep inside me I felt a spasm of fear.

Or was it a kick?

Minutes later Mossy had managed to cut a hole big enough for us all to clamber through, and then we were in. They appeared to be surprisingly organised for hippies, with the rainbow-dolphin guy – who answered to the name of Mango – producing a set of walkie-talkies. He handed one to Dustin. 'I'll stay as look out,' he whispered, waving us on. 'One blast for amber. Two for red.' As we crept through the undergrowth towards a set of outbuildings I turned to Dustin. 'What does he mean, amber and red?' 'Amber means someone's coming. We need to freeze or hide.' We carried on, the bush gradually thinning out. 'And red?' I asked.

'Red means we're fucked.'

We carried on, pushing our way deeper into the base, losing people as we went until finally it was just me, Dustin and Mossy left. 'Why do we need so many look-outs? There's no one here,' I asked as we paused for a moment behind a small Portakabin. 'Shhhh!' Mossy clamped a finger to her lips, gesturing across the courtyard. I scanned the windows of the buildings, confused about what I was supposed to be looking at. And then I saw them.

Up ahead were about a dozen soldiers, their heavy boots glinting in the mid-day sun. Two of the soldiers were clinging onto leads. Leads that were connected to dogs. Big, drooling German shepherds – the kind that consider hippies a tasty source of nutrients. I turned to Dustin for advice but he wasn't saying anything, the blood having leached from his face. Then I felt an urgent tug on my back as Mossy pulled me to my knees. 'Go, go, go!' she hissed, and next thing I knew the three of us were crawling through the scrubby grass, my heart pounding, my head pirouetting as I followed the gelatinous snake of Mossy's enormous behind.

Eventually we reached another fenced area, this one fringed with a serrated tinsel of razor wire, a cluster of yellow signs strung from the spikes. Danger of Death *and* Warning! Electricity! *I suddenly decided this was a very bad idea. 'This is the place,' Mossy said, handing me the walkie-talkie. 'If I'm not back in two minutes go back and meet the others.' And with that she was gone, dipping round the side of the enclosure and out of sight.*

I looked over at Dustin. He still hadn't said anything, his cheeks now flushed red from the exertion of the crawl. 'Are you alright?' I asked gently. He nodded once, not looking up. From somewhere beyond the fence there was a loud bang followed by a crunching of metal. I decided now was as good a time as any.

'Hey guess what? I'm pregnant… '

This time Dustin did look up. I don't know why I came out with it like that, but it worked. Dustin's face crinkled with confusion as his mouth desperately tried to form an appropriate response.

wooooooOOOOOOOoooow-woooooOOOOOOoooooow

An alarm started screaming from somewhere deep inside the enclosure, drowning out whatever Dustin had or hadn't managed to say. The next moment Mossy appeared, sprinting towards us, no longer even bothering to whisper.

'FUCKING RUN!'

We didn't need to be told twice. Still hanging onto the walkie-talkie – which by now was crackling with yells of 'Red Alert!' – I got my head down and started pumping my arms and legs, sprinting back in the direction we had crawled from. I thought I heard the snarl of angry dogs snapping in the distance, accompanied by the yells of even angrier men, but I didn't look behind me to find out if I was right. I just kept running, desperate to keep going, to escape. The world disappeared in a blur of adrenaline until finally all I could hear was the pounding of my heart in my chest as I put one foot in front of another.

Thump, thump, thump.

We hung around at The Bumpkin for hours afterwards, swapping stories of the raid, laughing about how scared we had been, slapping each other on the back. The attack had been a resounding success – the base already besieged by the reporters we'd tipped off in advance, who were now gleefully interrogating Air Force executives live on TV about the lax security and showing close-ups of Mossy's clumsily sprayed 'Troops out!' on the generator door. Everyone apart from me was drunk, with Dustin predictably hammered. But for once I didn't care. We were all brothers and sisters now. Dustin, Mossy, Mango and the rest of them. We hugged each other, squeezed each other around the waist. We had done it. We had actually done it.

I was still floating when I got back to my apartment later that evening, having finally waved goodbye to my new friends and left Dustin to sleep off the celebrations under a table at the back of The Bumpkin. As I made my way up the stairs, all I could think about was collapsing into bed. I don't think I've ever been so exhausted, yet I couldn't stop replaying the events of the day over and over again in my head. I still couldn't believe we'd actually pulled it off. Sure it might only have been a tiny victory, but it was a victory nevertheless. For the first time in my life,

I'd made a difference.

Swinging open the door, I noticed a small brown envelope lying on the mat, out of place amongst the stack of bills and takeaway leaflets that were usually jammed through my letter box. I turned the letter over in my hands, noticing first the address, printed in a child-like scrawl, then the brightly coloured foreign stamps. My stomach lurched. I tore the envelope open:

Hey Sugar Tits,

You said to write so here it is.

It's hot here. The food's bad and my feet are tired from all the walkin.

It ain't like on TV, I'll tell ya that for nothin.

I'm bad at writin and I ain't got much to say so I'll keep it short. I jus' wanted to let ya know that I'm getting a promotion. They're bumpin me up to Corporal already – I know, crazy huh? Apparently I show potential ha. It's more responsibility for only a little more money, but I think it could be good. For us I mean.

Anyway, I'm still not sure when I'm comin back. Could be a week, could be a month, they keep messin the date around. Who knows – I might even beat this letter back. The post out here's a joke.

Miss your sweet ass
Danny

I read the letter and re-read it. Danny's writing was as coarse and careless as his speech. It was strange having that voice in the apartment again after so many months alone. I took a seat by the window, reading the letter for a third time, trying to work up some emotion; excitement, disappointment – anything other than numb indifference.

I sat by the window a long time with the letter in my hand, not thinking, not feeling. Just sitting. When I finally moved I was surprised to find that it was night. I left the lights off as I made my way to the bedroom, climbing into bed fully dressed and pulling the blankets over my head, the darkness slowly swallowing me.

* * *

Everythin was black. The sand, the sky. Day and night. Me. I couldn't tell where things ended or began. In fact callin it black don't really do it justice, son. It was like when you stare into the mouth of a cave and you don't see nothin there – jus' emptiness starin right back at ya. I kept expectin my eyes to adjust any minute, but they never did. I blinked once, twice. Nothin. After a while I realised the reason I couldn't see nothin is because there weren't nothin to see. I couldn't tell ya how long I'd been waitin either. Might've been a coupla seconds. Could've been a coupla years. Shit, I didn't even know what I was waitin *for*. All I knew was that I was waitin. I figured I might be a while, so to pass the time I started countin.

1,2,3,4,5…

Once when I was a kid I had a fever so bad my ma thought I was gonna die. It started out in the morning as an ear infection, but by evenin I was burnin up. They called the doctor but he said I was too far gone – that I would probably slip into a coma, and that even if by some miracle I woke, I'd be retarded. There was nothin to do but strip me down and wait it out. For two days I lay and writhed in my sheets while Ma dabbed my brow with ice water and Pops smoked cigars and rang through the phone book for the cheapest coffin. On the third mornin the fever broke, but when I finally managed to sit up I had no idea who I was. I mean it, I didn't know my name, my age, nothin. Course it turned out the amnesia was only temporary, and by lunchtime I was back to my old self. Still, I remember how strange it felt for those few hours while

I sat hunched at the edge of my bed, waitin to come back to life. I guess I felt the way a baby feels when it first arrives in the world. No past or future to fuck you up. Just one endless present, stretchin on and on and on and on and on…

… 5026, 5027, 5028, 5029…

At some point I became aware of a sound, a low buzzin, like a wasp trapped in a jar. I looked around for the source of the noise, but of course I couldn't see nothin. I kept very still and tried to concentrate. It seemed that the sound was comin from somewhere high above my head – wherever my head was, ha. As I listened I realised the sound was gettin louder, getting closer. Suddenly I was afraid. I tried to block it out, to focus on the numbers, but it was no good.

… 12456, 12457, 12458, 12…

… I lost count. The sound was everywhere now, surroundin me, *inside* me even. It was around this time I realised I was floatin. Course I still couldn't see anythin, but somehow I knew I was no longer on the ground. It was like bein underwater, stuck at the bottom of a very deep, very dark lake. And somehow I'd managed to break free. The nothingness all around me began to flicker, from black to grey to brown to red. I tried to kick where I thought my legs should be, forcin my way upwards, desperate to make it to the surface. As I began to rise the sound got even louder, muffled by the water but nonetheless recognisable. It was a person. I was getting closer…

Up

Up

Up

At first I thought it was your mother, yellin at me for something I had or hadn't done. I tried callin her but I couldn't find my mouth. What the hell was wrong with her? Couldn't she see I was drownin here? She could at least give me a hand. And still I kept risin.

Up

Up

Up

I was nearly at the surface now, the voice almost close enough to make out the words. I decided it definitely wasn't your mother. I dunno why. Too concerned maybe. But if not her, then who? I peered up and saw the darkness had completely cleared. Distorted shapes rippled jus' above my head. The surface.

Up

Up

Up

Suddenly it all made sense. It was your voice, son. You were here to meet me. I tried to shout, I really did. I wanted to explain everythin to you. The war, your mother – me. I wanted to tell you that even though the world's a miserable piece of shit where bad things happen to good people almost as often as good things happen to the bad, a place where nothin turns out the way you expected and only fools believe in truth and hope and luck… that despite all of that, there is still such a thing as love. I know that now. Because I love you. And I'm sorry.

I wanted to tell you. I did. But when I opened my mouth all that came out was bubbles.

Up

Up

And…

Splash. The light was a shock. After being in the dark for so long I could hardly see. It felt like I had salt in my eyes. I tried to take a breath but the air stung my lungs. I gasped-coughed-gasped, bringin up half the ocean onto my lap. I spat a web of drool. I was alive. Then I remembered. The voice. It was softer now, almost a whisper, right in my ear. I blinked, once, twice, the world developin like an old fashioned photo. Until finally I saw who was speakin to me. And it wasn't you son. It wasn't even your mother.

It was God.

And she was a fuckin rag-head.

* * *

We were on the road again, preparing to smash the system, to fight the good fight.

Whatever that meant.

Dustin arrived before daybreak, collecting me up in his gleaming Prius and then hurtling down the deserted roads towards the coast. I pressed my face to the window as we drove, watching the city unravel into the suburbs until we finally reached the motorway, the grey geometric lines in stark contrast to the tangle of emotions I was struggling to make sense of. I unwound the glass a little, letting some air in to keep me awake and clear my head.

'Look, there it is! I win!' Dustin suddenly yelled, breaking the silence. 'I can see the sea! I can see the sea!'

I lifted my head and caught a snatch of grey in the distance, shimmering in the early dawn light. The ocean. I had no idea what we were doing there. 'Dustin,' I said. 'I know you've probably explained this to me a hundred times already, but just remind me again. Why are we going to the seaside?'

'Ah-ha... ' said Dustin.

We were going to see a man about a boat.

By the time we arrived at the docks, rush hour had already begun, the first snarl of traffic clogging the narrow roads. We dumped the van in a decrepit multi-storey car park and walked down to the water. Even though Dustin hadn't mentioned anything about my pregnancy since the raid on the airbase, I was acutely aware of my tummy. It had ballooned over the last week, forcing me to hide under layers of baggy t-shirts and thick jumpers, despite the heat. Jamming my hands into my pockets to further conceal my bump, I did my best to follow Dustin's rambling commentary.

'According to Jeremy, there's a secret naval operation going on here that's not being reported by the mainstream press.'

'Naval operation?' I asked. 'But there's no sea in the desert.'

'Ah, but they're not going to the desert. At least the boats aren't. They're planning to send an aircraft carrier to the gulf – that way they can send troops and supplies over in helicopters and... well the point is they're docking here this morning to refuel before they set out. It'll be a perfect opportunity to get ourselves noticed.'

'What, like on TV?' I asked, suddenly nervous.

'Exactly. You ever see those Greenpeace campaigners going after the whaling boats? It'll be like that. All we need to do is attach ourselves to the side of the boat and... Fuck.' Dustin stopped dead as we reached the foot of the pier.

'What... ?' I started, but then I spotted what it was Dustin was looking at. Spread out before us was an endless grey slab of ocean, stretching as far as the eye could see. Even though it was still early, there were already boats out on the water. Little tugs full of rugged, weather beaten fishermen, relics from another time; the odd cruiser taking handfuls of hopeful tourists out to view the coast or to try and spot dolphins. But Dustin wasn't looking at any of them. Instead he was staring at the horizon, at the silhouette of a large warship travelling east to west.

Away from the shore.

'Fuck, fuck, fuck – what time is it?'

I fumbled in my layers, trying to find my phone. 'Seven.'

'Shit – it's not supposed to leave until nine. I don't believe it!'

We stood there watching as the boat turned into a distant speck and then disappeared completely. Dustin turned back to me and sighed. 'Well, that was a colossal balls up. Still now that we're here we might as well make a day of it. Fancy an ice cream?

It was one of those crumbling Victorian seaside towns, a vaguely disconcerting mixture of charity shops and off-licences jostling for space in the fading majesty of the old plaza. Everyone we passed was old – folded up and wheelchair bound. The air smelled of salt and cigarettes and unchanged incontinence pads. It was a place people came to die. As it turned out it was still too early to find anywhere that would sell us ice cream so we had to make do with Snickers bars from a vending machine outside the local penny arcade. We ate and walked, taking in the sights as we went. It didn't take long, and within half an hour we were back at the beach.

As we stood there, watching the sea collapse against the stony shore, Dustin suddenly turned to me, 'So tell me about Danny.'

He made it sound so casual, almost as if it had just popped into his head right then, rather than something that had been eating him up ever since that night at the Tokyo Lucky Hole. 'What do you want to know?' I asked, struggling to keep the note of irritation from my voice.

'Well, I just can't get my head around it. There you are – this young, intelligent woman... admittedly with a self-destructive streak. But a soldier? Really? It just doesn't make sense.'

I stood there, listening to the roar then tinkle of the waves lapping at the stony shore. It took me a long time to answer. 'Just because he's a soldier doesn't make him a bad person. I mean... I might not agree with what he's fighting for but at least he's fighting... '

'But so are we!' said Dustin, taking a step towards me. 'And at least what we're fighting for is worth something, is real. I mean – are you even happy?'

I reached down and launched a pebble across the water, watching it bounce-bounce-bounce then sink without a trace. And then I exploded, my anger stunting my sentences. 'Do you know the thing I hate about you Dustin? Well, there are lots of things really – but the thing I hate the most? It's that you're so sure that you're right. It's Dustin's way or the highway. And life isn't like that, you know? It's great to have ideals but... Life isn't black and white! You're this privileged middle-class guy and yet you roam around acting like, like... You're just so sickeningly, disgustingly self-righteous...

You're, you're… a pig!'

Dustin stood there for a moment, not looking at me. In the distance a seagull screeched, a dog barked. Up on the pier an old man stood hunched over his walker, willing the world to put him out of his misery.

And then Dustin leant forward and kissed me.

And I kissed him back.

* * *

Her name was Afsaneh, but she let me call her Afa. At least she did once I'd learnt how to talk again. Seems the explosion had knocked out a coupla teeth, as well as bustin my ribs and leavin a huge gash on my leg that wept thick yellow pus all day and itched to high hell all night. I guess you could say I was bent outta shape. Her English was bad but good enough to explain I'd been unconscious for three days. She also managed to fill in some of the blanks about how I'd ended up there. 'Goat… blow up,' she said as she bent over me to change my bandages. 'My sister find you when she look for wood... bring you here.' Her breath was warm, with an undertang of bad meat. It was the sweetest thing I've ever smelt. 'What about Cal?' I tried to ask through my swollen gums. 'Jett? What about my friends?' Either she didn't understand or she didn't know because she didn't answer me, instead movin further down the bed to dress my leg. I closed my eyes and when I opened them again she was gone.

After a few days I began to get a bit of strength back and started to look round the room. In my fever I'd assumed I was in a hospital, but sittin up I realised it was actually in some sort of shack, the walls a patchwork of rustin corrugated steel sheets, holes plugged with balls of yellow newspaper and the odd plank of wood nailed haphazardly around the place to provide support. My bed turned out to be little more than a faded carpet folded over a coupla old wooden crates, with a few rags of linen dangling down on either side, presumably to deter mosquitoes. Most importantly though, there was a jug within reach, which Afa kept topped up with warm, slightly salty water. It tasted like piss, but I didn't care. I drank 'til I nearly drowned.

One morning Afa came in and set a plate of food next to me, some sort of mashed root vegetable I didn't recognise with a small pile of grey meat next to it. It was the first thing I'd eaten for weeks and I didn't even stop to thank her as I shovelled the flavourless mush into my mouth. Afa seemed to linger a little longer than usual, a strange smile ticklin the corners of her mouth as she watched me eat. She was a funny-lookin thing, her dark face dominated by these huge almond eyes, almost as black as the few strands of hair that poked out from under her headscarf. She weren't pretty exactly – she had a pin in her nose for one thing and I've always hated that shit – but still, there was somethin about her. I had no idea how old she was. She had the slight, springy frame of a teenager, and at first glance I'd put her at sixteen or seventeen. Yet as she stood there watchin me eat I noticed there was somethin in her face that made her look much, much older. I guess it's difficult to tell with wogs.

When I'd finished eatin she took the plate from my lap but carried on waitin there, that little smile near 'nuff drivin me crazy. 'Well, spit it out,' I snapped, already a little stoned from the food. Afa's eyes lit up. 'Wait here,' she said, and scurried off towards the door. Like I was gonna go anywhere. A little while later I heard a loud scrapin noise, as if somethin heavy were bein dragged across the floor of the shack. I looked over to see Afa bent down next to a girl I'd never seen before, a tiny, bird-like thing, definitely younger but with the same big dark eyes as Afa. I craned my neck to see what it was they were draggin but I couldn't make it out through the tangle of brightly coloured shawls. After a coupla minutes they finally had the thing level with me. They stepped aside with a flourish, as if presentin me with some sorta Christmas gift. I looked and looked again, tryna work out what in fuck's name I was supposed to be lookin *at*.

At first I thought it was a giant lump of meat – like one of them grizzled hunks of kebab you see skewered in the windows of Turkish restaurants, only it was wrapped tightly in a clean cotton sheet and propped up in a sort of makeshift wheelchair. I scratched my head. It was too much to eat, even for the three of us. Maybe it was Christmas after all. Then the kebab opened its mouth and spoke.

'Private Calthorpe reportin for duty, Sir,' it said.

It was Cal.

The girls left us to catch up. It took at least an hour to get things straightened out, and even then I'm not sure we got anywhere. Considerin how bad his face was, Cal's speech was remarkably clear, though the truth was I could barely stand to look at him he was so mangled up. Gettin him to stay on point was another matter altogether. He seemed to have developed a habit of stoppin halfway through a sentence and starin off into the distance, or laughin hysterically, coverin his BBQ-charred hands and wheezin like a busted accordion. He kept changin the subject too, one second talkin about how he can't move the fingers on his left hand and the next about a family holiday to France he'd been on when he was six. I guess it wasn't only his face that was fried.

Anyway, in the end I managed to piece most of it together. Like Afa had said, the goat had been booby-trapped – Cal explained it was a simple explosive device packed with nails and other assorted shrapnel. Gita, the other girl who'd come in with Afa and who'd been lookin after Cal, had removed about fourteen pieces from his face, including a ring pull from a can of Coke that was embedded in his jaw. She'd explained to him that these kind of devices were popular with the local rebels, sorta like a walkin proximity mine. The bell round the goat's neck was a warnin to keep away.

Jett was killed instantly of course. Apparently there weren't enough of him left to be worth bringin back. Lookin at Cal, I couldn't work out if it'd been worth bringin him back either. Apart from the burns, he seemed to have lost most of his nose, as well as three fingers on one hand. I didn't ask to see underneath the sheet. Compared to him I guess I'd gotten off pretty lightly.

'So what?' I said when Cal had finished speaking. 'This sand nigger just happened to be out gatherin wood when she stumbled across our sorry asses?' Cal nodded. The village we were in now was less than two miles away from where we'd first seen the goat. After findin us lyin in the dirt she'd run back to raise the alarm, only to find half the village was already on its way. They buried what was left of Jett, loaded us onto an old wooden cart and dragged us back to the hospital to patch us up. We'd been here ever since.

I took a second to again glance around the dingy wooden shack. 'Some hospital, huh?' Cal chuckled. 'Still, beats bleedin to death.' I nodded, unsure whether I agreed or not. 'And this Gita, she explained all this to you?' Cal's smile faded. 'Sorta.' 'Sorta?' Cal looked down. 'Her English ain't too hot. But you see the thing is Sir, I weren't exactly unconscious while all of it was happenin. I remember lyin there, right after it happened. It was freezin cold, even with the sun shinin. And I remember seein Jett. The look on his face. He didn't even look human. It was… it was… '

As if on cue Gita and Afa reappeared at the door. 'Ok visiting time over now. Mister Cal needs his sleep.' I nodded. 'Gita's right buddy. You need to rest up.' I turned back to the girls. 'Actually, I've been meanin to ask you. Do you have a phone we could use?' She looked at me blankly, while Cal started giggling idiotically, little snorts fartin outta the flap where his nose used to be. 'They ain't got no phones! They ain't even got electricity!' he squealed. I shrugged, 'Ok, don't worry about it. Listen Cal, we're gonna get you fixed up nice and good and then we'll hit the road again. There must be hundreds of villages round here – one of them's bound to have a phone. We can call the base and let them know our location and… ' I trailed off as Cal's laughter became hysterical, his giggles cascading over into a sickenin rasp. He sounded like he was about to fuckin drown.

As the girls bent down and started to drag him out of the room, Cal stopped laughin abruptly and stared at me, a manic grin stretched across his deformed face. Wordlessly he leant forward and parted the sheet that was wrapped around the lower half of his body. 'Yep! We'll jus' hit the road Sir!' he said, startin to laugh again.

That's when I understood what was so funny.

Because underneath the sheet, right where his legs should've been, weren't nothin but two bloody stumps.

* * *

You kicked and the world crumbled.

For the first few days after the beach I bounced about in a hermetically sealed daze. I'd spent the long drive home nestled into Dustin's shoulder and when he pulled up outside his crumbling maisonette I followed him inside without resistance. It felt good to be led like that, to be given no choice. For the first time I started to see the appeal of Danny's job.

Dustin's house wasn't at all what I'd been expecting. Yes it was sleek and modern, with a disconcerting number of chrome-plated kitchen appliances, but there was a warmth to the place. Piles of books competed for space with empty bottles of wine on every surface, half-smoked joints nestled in ashtrays. Compared to the sterile order of my place, it felt alive. The kind of place you could call home.

Dustin fetched me a cup of peppermint tea and put on some jazz in the background while I snuggled down amongst the expensive clutter of his universe.

I didn't leave for two days.

Eventually Dustin admitted he should probably go and do some work, reluctantly leaving me curled up in his bed. After another hour's sleep I got up and went home to pick up some fresh clothes, tired of slumming around in Dustin's oversized t-shirt. As I opened the apartment door a flood of familiar smells greeted me – faint non-specific odours that brought an avalanche of memories. Swallowing down my guilt I went through to the bedroom to start packing an overnight bag.

And that's when you decided to say hello.

It was only the smallest nudge but it literally floored me, sending me sinking to my knees as I clutched my belly. I don't know why I was so surprised. I'd been carrying you around for nearly twenty weeks, yet for a few days I'd allowed myself to forget about everything. I touched my face, surprised to find I was crying, though I wasn't sure why. Maybe it's because I knew it was over with Dustin. From that second I knew I could never go back. I had other things to think about. Duties. Something I had to nourish and protect. I decided to call him right away.

'Heyyyy, you've reached Dustin. You're talking to a machine… '

I decided not to leave a message. Whatever I was going to say, I would say it to his face. I owed him that at least.

I spent the rest of the day moping around the apartment, occasionally trying to call again but getting nowhere. I drafted a couple of letters to give him instead, but it was no good. I felt stupid every time. Plus my brain didn't seem to be working, everything thick and foggy and underwater. I wondered if this was what life would be like from now on – whether that was the big secret no one told you about babies. I thought of all the desperate zombie-eyed mums I'd seen shuffling around Save the Animals, clutching their offspring to their grossly distended bosom, barely able to string a sentence together beyond the next nappy. Was that my future? Had the madness already set in?

I decided I needed to get some air.

I walked aimlessly for around half an hour, yet somehow I found myself on the same road as Save the Animals. However, when I got closer I saw the shutter was down and the lights were off. I tried Dustin again, the sound of his voicemail ringing in my ear for the hundredth time that day. I found myself growing quietly furious. After all, I was the one doing the dumping here, not the other way round.

I was halfway down the street before I realised I was on my way to his house.

After knocking on the door for maybe ten minutes, I started seriously considering climbing onto his balcony to press my face against his bedroom window. In the end though, I decided I was probably overreacting. Knowing Dustin he'd probably bumped into an old friend and gone for a drink. The best thing to do was to go home and wait for him to call – it wasn't like I was short of things to be getting on with.

And so, putting Dustin as far as I could out of my mind, I spent the next few days clearing out the spare bedroom, transforming the drab space into a yellow nest of cotton blankets and folded baby grows. I still didn't have a crib but I figured Danny would be home soon and we could...

Well, who knew? Maybe things would be better this time.

Stranger things had happened.

After I'd finished decorating the nursery I retreated to my bedroom, building a pillow fortress and camping out with a book, trying to read but spending most of my time staring at the ceiling, determined not to look at my phone. I must have fallen asleep because when I woke it was dark. Sitting up, I realised I was ravenous. Racking my brain to recall what supplies I had in the fridge, I checked my phone and saw I had a text message.

MEET ME AT THE SHOP TONIGHT 9. DUSTIN.

The message was ten minutes old. I tried calling him back but it went straight to answerphone again. Fucking Dustin. It was already 8.45. There was no way I'd make it in time. Anyway, why should I go? It's not like he'd made any effort before now. Three days without so much as a word? He could be dead for all I know, and now he was back in touch without so much as a sorry. There was no way I was going meet him. Absolutely no chance…

I squeezed into my largest pair of jeans and waddled down the hall.

I opened the front door.

And started running.

I was gasping by the time I reached the shop. I've never been particularly fit, but the pregnancy seemed to have drained what microscopic reserves of energy I had. I took a second to catch my breath and compose myself, desperately hoping I wasn't about to get sick. I rehearsed my lines, ready to confront him. I wasn't even going to get angry. I was just going to lay it down, tell it exactly how it was.

It's over.

I rattled the metal shutter, reaching through the bars to tap the glass. The light that had been on in the back instantly clicked off, shortly followed by a loud crunch as the steel frame slowly started to lift. It seemed to take forever. I pictured myself turning and running down the street. But I didn't move. Dustin owed me an explanation, if nothing else.

Finally the shutter disappeared altogether and I heard the rattle of keys in the glass. I tapped my foot impatiently, needing yet another wee. I decided I needed to make this as quick and as painless as possible. In and out.

The door opened.

But it wasn't Dustin standing there.

It was Jeremy.

* * *

Weeks passed and every day I got stronger. Afa kept fillin the jug with salty water and bringin through the plates of mush and I kept drinkin and eatin until eventually my ribs stopped achin and the cut on my leg stopped weepin and formed a smooth, shiny scab. I slept a lot too – proper sleep, like I hadn't in years, untroubled by visions or bad dreams. It felt good, like someone throwin their arms around me and holdin me to their chest. Safe, secure. I woke up feelin calm and refreshed.

One day I was finishin up eatin when I realised I was well enough to get out of bed and take a look around. Settin the plate carefully on the side, I swung my legs tentatively over the side of the bed and limped over to the doorway. The light stung my eyes as I peeled back the curtain and made my way out into a small, dusty courtyard. It was funny; for some reason I'd imagined a large village, sort of a rag-head version of our F.O.B., but as I wandered round the dilapidated square I saw that it wasn't the case. There were maybe eight buildings in total, arranged in a loose rectangle, though to be honest, callin them buildings was probably pushin it a little. Just like my 'hospital', they were little more than corrugated steel shacks, though even for a shanty town they were in a bad state, with rust holes yawnin in the sides of the houses and overlappin sheets of metal patched with duct tape markin out multiple botched repairs. Yup, it was a mess alright.

As I stood there tryin to figure out which buildin Cal might be stayin in, I heard a noise behind me and turned to see a small, dirty-lookin child chasin after an underinflated football. Sensin somebody watchin, the kid paused mid-kick and looked up at me. He was nervous, but not particularly surprised – the same way you might look if someone'd warned you about rattlesnakes right after one cornered you in your bedroom. Instinctively I raised my hand and waved. All of a sudden the kid jumped to life. Shit, you'd think I'd pulled a gun on him he moved so quick, abandonin his crushed ball and tearin away from me, duckin down behind one of the tin houses and out of sight. I stood there blinkin. The only people I'd seen apart from Afa was Cal and Gita, though I'd guessed from the noises that there must be more. Still, I hadn't counted on there bein children out here. For some reason it didn't seem right.

I was still standin there when Afa came outta one of the

houses, laughin brightly with Gita. As she caught sight of me, her expression turned serious, 'Mr Danny… you need rest.' I grinned, swattin her away. 'I'm fine, really. Jus' stretchin my legs is all.' Noddin uncertainly, she turned back to Gita and whispered something in her ear before leavin her to come and join me. 'Then I will stretch your legs as well.'

We walked in a large circle around the outside of the village, stoppin now and then for Afa to point out various features to me. The place was actually much bigger than I'd first thought. Apart from the central settlement of shacks, there was a large stretch of scrubland that sprawled for maybe a half mile that apparently served as an allotment. Anaemic-lookin plants swooned next to dry irrigation trenches. I didn't recognise much of what was growin apart from a few species of edible cactus and a handful of shrivelled grapes hangin limply from a splinterin trellis. 'They need water,' I said to Afa. She turned to me, a silther of sadness in her smile. 'We all need water.'

We kept walkin, past the allotment to a small, cracked dust-bowl with a pen containin three or four emaciated goats. 'This used to be lake. Long time ago. Now we only have well.' She pointed back towards the village. 'The water no good. It salty. We have to heat, but it takes a long time.' I nodded, thinkin about the bottomless jugs of water by the side of my bed. Just then it occurred to me to ask her somethin I'd been ponderin for a while. 'Hey Afa, how'd you come to speak English so good?' She stopped and shook her head. 'Maybe I ask how you come to speak English so bad, huh?'

I grinned, but before I could answer there was a loud scream as two more children fell out from behind a rock and started runnin back towards the village. Afa yelled somethin after them I didn't understand. The children ran faster. 'They were spying on you,' she explained. 'They no seen a soldier before. They think you might be a Monster.' 'What did you tell them?' I asked. Afa grinned. 'I said you'd eat them up if you caught them spying again.'

As we walked back towards the square Afa told me her story. She'd lived in the village her whole life. Twenty years she said, though I think their calendar is slightly different from ours. Her father had been a member of a nomadic tribe – people who'd lived for centuries trading camels and spices, back when it wasn't just children who'd never seen a soldier or a Monster. When he met her mother they decided to settle, pickin a spot close to the water and invitin her mother's extended family to live with them. They grew crops and farmed goats and said their prayers five times a day. They worked hard but were happy; their throats full of laughter and their bellies full of food. They raised a family. Then one day, around five years ago, everythin changed.

The farm had been strugglin for a while – the lake had been getting shallower with each increasingly hot summer, until now barely a muddy puddle remained, forcin them to drill down to the salty reserves that ran deep beneath. The same crops that'd bloomed only the year before started to wither and die. The goats' ribs started to show through their skin. Then one summer the harvest failed altogether. Her father couldn't understand it. He prayed harder and longer each day, lookin to the sky for rain, but the sun just kept on shinin. They ate what little food they had stored until it ran out. Still the sun shone. They began to starve. Afa's father continued to pray, head bowed in submission, kneelin in the sand from morning until night until his skin blistered and his hair went white, but still there was no rain. Then one day her mother took sick and died and Afa's father stopped prayin altogether. He decided to make a miracle happen for himself.

Roundin up four of their remainin six goats, Afa's father took a ceremonial blade and slaughtered them in the centre of the village, makin a point of not makin a sacrifice. After he had carefully skinned them and stretched the hides out to dry, he called for Afa's two older brothers to help tie them to the camels. They were to travel with him to the market. Afa cried and begged for them to stay, but her father was adamant

– they would all die if he didn't go. Besides, he would be back in three days.

I felt sick. 'So what happened?'

'That was three months ago,' Afa said. 'He's never returned. A week after he left the rains came. It seems God always steps in to save us right when we need it the most.' 'And now?' I asked, thinkin of the brown grapes, the empty lake. 'Where is God now?' Afa smiled, her eyes flashin defiantly. 'Well, He sent you along, didn't He?'

More weeks passed, and I began to settle into my new life at the village. I spent the mornin working on the farm and lookin after the goats. I figured after all the help Afa had given me it was a fair exchange. Plus it helped pass the time while I figured out what I was gonna do with Cal.

There weren't a whole bunch I could do to fix the lack of water – it took at least an hour of work at the well to fill even a jug – but by diggin the irrigation trenches a little deeper I was at least able to make sure what little water we had went further. Apart from that I spent my time weedin and prunin the crops, snappin off the dead leaves to encourage the smaller green shoots to grow, riggin up a web of linen from wooden plinths to protect the young plants from the harsh mid-day sun. Afa worked alongside me most days, bringin with her an army of little children, who by now had lost all fear of me, climbin on my back or clingin to my legs whenever they got bored of workin. There was eight of them in total, all girls apart from one boy, Basim, Afa's youngest brother. The kid was only six, a scruffy slip of a thing with these huge brown eyes and this cheeky smile. Monkey I called him, always fightin with his sisters or climbin things. Sorta reminded me of you if I'm honest.

At midday we would return to the square and eat together, the portions havin become noticeably smaller since I'd left the hospital, before spendin the afternoons helpin the kids at 'school' – which basically consisted of singin, tellin stories and chasin after Basim. Afa usually got me to tell the children a story from my life 'across the sea' – she said it would help them with their English, but to be honest I'm not convinced they understood a word of what I was sayin. Still, they sat in rapt silence whenever I spoke, eyeballin me like I was some sort of alien high priest, hangin on my every word. In the evenings I would return to my little shack and lie on my bunk, where to my surprise sleep found me without difficulty.

One night I woke to find Afa had crept into my room and curled up next to me, her bird-boned body pushed up against mine, her hair fallin over my eyes like a thin black curtain. In the mornin she was gone, and when I made it down to the farm I found her there, already hard at work. She didn't say a word to me about it and the day passed as normal, but that night I woke again to find her next to me. From then on we fell into a pattern, with her silently sneakin into my bed halfway through the night, always careful to leave before first light. All we ever did was lie there, alone together under the roof of my shack. The next day neither of us would utter a word about it. Not once. Still, in its own way it was more intense, more intimate, than all of the fuckin I'd done in my life added up. After a while it got so I wouldn't bother goin to sleep until she arrived. I'd just lie there in the dark, waitin.

* * *

Jeremy stood in the shadows, waiting.

'Come in and don't say anything. You may have been followed.'

I stepped inside the shop and Jeremy locked the door behind me. I waited for a moment for Dustin to leap out from behind the counter and surprise me, but one glance at Jeremy's face told me this was no joke. 'Where's Dustin? He said he'd meet me here.'

'Take a seat Lorna,'

'What's going on?' I asked, but I sat down anyway, perching on a stool next to a stack of ancient board games.

Jeremy hovered by the window for a while, flinching slightly every time a car passed before eventually turning back to face me. 'There's been an unforeseen complication... '

I glanced up at him. His blond hair was hanging limply over his face, the shadows making him look even thinner and more angular than usual. I saw he was holding something in his hand. A mobile phone. 'You texted me?' I asked, panic rushing to close my throat. 'But it was... Dustin wanted me to... '

'Dustin asked me to make sure you were safe. I met him and he gave me his phone.'

'Where is he?' I demanded, standing up to face Jeremy. 'I'm not scared of you. I'll call the police.' Jeremy sighed and slipped the phone back into his pocket. 'Did Dustin ever talk to you about us? About Project Clearwater?' I shook my head. 'I know he was involved in... things. The airbase. The boat... ' 'I'm not talking about petty acts of vandalism,' Jeremy snapped. 'Do you remember the videos we showed you? They were part of a larger strategy. Dustin was a key player in the delivery of that strategy... '

'Was?' *I asked. 'As in he isn't anymore?'*

Outside a car screeched past, its headlights spilling into the room for a second before we were once again plunged into darkness. Jeremy glanced uneasily at the window before continuing. 'Dustin understood the risks. He knew that Project Clearwater was a vital step in securing peace and stopping this bullshit war for good. He also left specific instructions should anything happen to him in the line of duty... ' I laughed, cold and hard. 'In the line of duty? Jesus, do you ever listen to yourself? This is somebody's life you're talking about. But you want to turn it into some tawdry little thriller. People don't just disappear.'

'Lorna I understand you're upset. But Dustin isn't coming back. Before he went he asked me to give you something. To help continue his work.' He paused and reached into his jacket, holding out something for me to take.

A memory stick.

'Dustin wanted you to have this.' 'What's on it?' I asked. 'You know what's on it. It's a copy of a copy. I want you to hold onto it just in case... Until the time is right. And then I want you to get it out there. Call the papers, the TV stations. Everyone. Just make sure people know.' 'Wait,' I said, desperately trying to gather my thoughts. 'Get it out there? Why can't you get it out there? And how will I know when the time is right?' Jeremy shrugged, already walking towards the door. 'Dustin said you'd know.' And with that he slid back the latch and held the door open for me.

I didn't move.

'Jeremy this is ridiculous. I mean, I'm not even part of this. Whatever this is. Dustin was obviously overreacting. If you just call him or something I'm sure...' Another car passed the shop, this time the headlights illuminating Jeremy's face. Below his lank fringe I saw the outline of a black eye, a split lip. 'You need to go Lorna. Now.' I started towards the door but Jeremy stopped me, holding out the memory stick.

'Please?'

I took it without a word, turning back as I got to the street. 'I still don't know what I'm supposed to do with this... ' But already the steel shutter had started to come down.

It was time to go.

All the way home I had the feeling I was being followed. Cars seemed to slow every time they passed, and I was convinced one was going to stop and bundle me inside. I could almost feel the bag being forced over my head, my hands being bound with cable-ties as I fingered the smooth plastic casing of the memory stick in my pocket. But none of the cars stopped, and as I got closer to my apartment I started to wonder whether Jeremy wasn't simply being paranoid. I mean, even Dustin had said Jeremy was theatrical. Wasn't it possible this was all some elaborate joke?

By the time I reached the apartment I'd pretty much reassured myself that everybody involved was overreacting – Jeremy and Dustin were running around playing stupid spy *games and I'd allowed myself to get dragged in. Honestly, there was probably nothing on the bloody stick apart from a copy of the James Bond soundtrack.*

Bloody men! Boys more like...

As I punched in the code for the door, I suddenly heard a noise close behind me. The slamming of a car door followed by quick footsteps. I scanned the drive but saw no one. I shook my head. It seemed the paranoia was catching. I turned back to the pad. My code wasn't working for some reason, a small red cross flashing up every time I punched the digits.

More footsteps.

This time I saw something when I turned. A flash of silver, over by the recycling bins. I stabbed the door code into the keypad again and again, the screen filling with little red crosses. Behind me I thought I heard the crackle of a walkie-talkie.

Maybe.

Instructions to move on the target.

Maybe.

Giving up on the keypad I started hitting random buzzers, waiting for the red sight of a sniper rifle to drift into my field of view.

For the world to disappear.

Instinctively my hand came up to my stomach – as if a few extra millimetres of flesh and bone could somehow halt the forward trajectory of a speeding bullet. I felt you kick in response.

Suddenly there was a click as the door swung open, someone in the block having unwittingly saved my life.

Wheezing for breath, I heaved myself up the stairs, not wanting to lose time waiting for the lift. As I hit the second floor I thought I heard the door swing open below me. Not waiting to find out if I was imagining things, I powered forward, slotting my key into the lock and twisting the handle. It opened first time and I tumbled inside, shoving the door shut behind me and then sinking to my knees.

It was only then I realised I was crying, my whole body shaking uncontrollably. Deep inside, I felt you go very still, as if you knew something was wrong.

Eventually I took a deep breath and clambered up to my feet, fumbling for the light switch. I never made it. Because at the bottom of the hallway, standing in the shadows, someone was watching me. And even in the darkness, I could see they were smiling.

'Hello Lorna.'

* * *

Yup, I'd have to say that those weeks I spent with Afa and Basim and the rest of 'em were about the most content I can remember. Sure we were hungry, and there was never enough of that salty water to go around, but there was comfort in the routine. I had work to do in the day and a good woman to hang onto at night. What more could a man reasonably hope for in this sorry-ass world? The only real problem was Cal.

It was weird – it seemed the stronger and happier I got, the more miserable and withdrawn he became. After a while it got so he wouldn't see anyone, especially not me. The only person he'd let near him was Gita, who'd bring him his meals while he sat festerin in his room. Now and again I'd ask her how he was doin but she'd jus' shrug and shake her head. 'It takes time.' Once a week Gita would manage to drag him out of the shack to walk him around the village for some fresh air. The kids would run and hide, terrified of his chewed up face, so Gita started takin him right out past the farm so as not to run into anybody. I'd wave to him if I ever saw him but he never waved back. I figured Gita was right. Maybe all he needed was time.

One mornin I was workin down on the farm. There was some sort of rag-head holy day comin up and the village was plannin a feast. That particular mornin it was jus' me and Basim, as Afa had taken the girls to start decoratin the school.

I'd decided to try and stake out some of the weaker veggies as they weren't strong enough to carry their own weight. It was a tricky job as we didn't have any wire, so instead I was gettin Basim to double up lengths of straw and tie them around my makeshift wooden spikes. We were about a third of the way through the job when the screamin began.

For a second I thought I was mistaken, that maybe it was a bird or somethin, but then I heard the poundin of footsteps and I looked up to see Afa sprintin towards me, her face a smear of pain and tears. 'Help!' she called as I ran to meet her. 'Come quick…. It's Gita… I think she's dying.' We ran in silence back to the village, little Basim pantin alongside us, trying to keep up. As we reached Gita's shack, Afa paused a second, blockin the door. 'Please… try and do something.' With that she quickly stepped aside to let me pass and then followed me into the room, pullin the curtain sharply behind her to shield Basim from the scene unfoldin inside.

Gita was lyin on the bed, moanin quietly under her breath. She was coddled in a thin sheet, her face contorted in pain. In the dim light I could just about make out a thick knot of towels bunched between her legs. The towels were stained red. I put an arm around Afa, but she shrugged it off. 'Your friend did this,' she said, noddin at Gita in disgust. 'Who, Cal?' I asked, genuinely surprised. 'The boy's in a damn wheelchair!' At the mention of his name, Gita let out a low moan. 'She was taking him for his walk,' Afa continued. 'He say he had something in his eye. When she looked he was holding knife. He took her, forced her…' At this Gita's moans became even louder. I glanced down at the small purple bruises already blossoming on her bony wrists. It looked like he'd broken her nose too. Oh Cal, you stupid fuck. 'Ok,' I sighed. 'Where is he now?' Afa shook her head. 'I don't know. Still there maybe? He didn't follow her back to the village.' 'I'll fix this,' I said, already backin towards the door. 'I'll find him and make it better, ok Gita? Let me do that for you.' Afa smiled bitterly. 'You do that,' she said.

'You find him and you *fix* him. And then you leave and never come back. You soldiers are all the same. You come and you take what you want and you don't care. You just take, take, take, until there's nothing.' 'I'll make it better,' I said again. But Afa had already turned her back on me.

As I stormed through the village I reached into my jacket to check my handgun. I'd decided against going back to my shack to pick up my rifle, which'd sat neglected under my bed since I'd arrived here. I checked the clip on the 9mm. I realised this was the first time I'd held it in my hands since the goat attack. There were three bullets left in the chamber.

When I reached the farm I scanned the horizon for signs of life, seein nothin but flies and goats. Afa had obviously managed to herd the children to the safety of the school. For once, even Basim wasn't snappin at my heels. I was alone. Suddenly there was a flicker of movement in the distance as Cal broke cover, wheelin himself further out into the desert. I reached for my gun and fixed him in my sights, my arm deadly still, my finger on the trigger. I paused. Three bullets. I couldn't risk it. Slippin my gun back into its holster, I started racin towards him, my freshly staked vegetables trampled under the weight of my boots.

I caught up with him easily, the small, make-shift wheelchair no match for the sandy terrain. When I was a few hundred yards from him he turned and spotted me, his arms flappin as he desperately tried to wheel himself faster. I swear to god it would've been funny if I wasn't about to blow his head off.

'Ok that's it Cal,' I called out. 'Fun's over.' He gave one last surge, his chair scrapin on a large rock, and then stopped, still facin away from me. I reached into my jacket. 'Bitch made me do it!' He called out, his thin, nasal voice echoin around the clearin. 'Fuckin bent over me every day, rubbin me, touchin me. She was askin for it.' My thumb hooked over the top of my gun, pulled back the safety. 'She didn't even get upset until afterwards,' Cal continued, his voice crackin now, though with laughter or tears I couldn't tell. 'Reckon she didn't mind it as well. Y'know how these blacks are – actin all coy and shit. I seen it in her eyes. She wanted it.'

I took a couple of steps towards him and held out my arm, linin up the back of his head with the gun. 'You know I'm going to shoot you now Cal?' I asked. 'That I don't have a choice.' I watched his shoulders tense up and begin to shake. Very slowly he started to wheel his chair around, until eventually he was facin me. Even with all those scars, he looked like a sad, scared kid.

'Oh fuck I'm so sorry Sir. I'm sorry, I'll do anythin. I was jus' so lonely and she was lookin at me and I swear she wanted it, she WANTED it. I'm SORRY!' He was disolvin before my eyes, like a tender steak stuck through the mincer, his tears tinged pink as the scabs started to open up, his face literally fallin apart. He was a mess, a pitiful, disgustin mess. And I was about to do him the only favour he had left comin to him. My finger stroked the trigger. 'I'm sorry too Cal.' He closed his eyes, a dark patch spreadin across the front of his trousers. His mouth twisted into a scream.

And then something happened.

There was a roar, not Cal screamin, but somethin else, louder and infinitely more powerful, shaking the earth beneath our feet. I span around and dropped to my knees, years of trainin kickin in. Muscle memory. The sound intensified, was everywhere, my ears buzzin, my teeth vibratin in their gums. And the weird thing was I weren't scared. Not one bit. Because this is what I was out here for, what I was made for.

Ignorin Cal completely now, I rolled over and took up a firin position on my belly, grippin my pistol firmly with both hands. I gritted my teeth and said my prayers. I was ready. We were under attack, and I'm tellin ya son – it felt great! Because finally, *finally*, we had found ourselves a Monster.

* * *

'Hello Lorna.'

Danny moved quickly towards me, still smiling – though the closer he got the more his smile began to resemble a grimace. I reached for the light switch again.

'Uh-uh,' he said, grabbing me by the wrist.

I smiled nervously, trying to pull away. His grip tightened. It was then I noticed the crumpled slip of paper in his hand, the sad, looping lines of a failed Dear Dustin letter gleaming like a death warrant.

Signed, sealed, delivered.

I'm yours.

Danny leant closer and pushed his teeth into my lips, a parody of a kiss. 'Surprised to see me huh? Only ya look a little outta sorts… '

'Danny, I can explain.'

Danny pulled back a couple of inches so that he was staring me in the eye. I could smell bourbon on his breath. Bourbon and hate. 'So explain,' he said calmly.

I took a breath. 'Dustin's a friend. A colleague, at the charity shop. And he got the wrong idea. I don't know, he was confused. We both were but... But you weren't here Danny. And even when you were, you weren't interested. I tried. I did. But you didn't want to know. And I was lonely. I don't think that makes me a bad person.' I heard my voice crack, the panic seeping into my speech. 'But, oh god, I don't know what the hell's going on anymore. Dustin was part of this group of activists and… I think I was followed home. I think something bad is going to happen. Something really, really… '

Crack!

The blow took me off my feet and onto the floor. At first I thought it was just the shock that had caused me to crumble, Danny's right fist seeming to swing out of nowhere, but when I put my hand to my face I knew at once my jaw was broken.

'Now,' Danny said, examining his knuckles. 'I don't wanna hear another goddamn sound come outta your cheatin fuckin trap. Do you understand?' His voice was level, bored almost

– as if he was trying to explain something to a naughty child. 'Do you understand?'

I nodded, whimpering slightly, my face pulsing with pain.

Thump!

This time Danny swung his leg back and caught me just below the knee. 'I said I didn't want to hear a sound.' He paused, smiling again. 'Now, have we got anything in the fridge?'

I didn't move.

'Cos I could eat a fuckin horse. Why don't you go to the bathroom and clean up and then cook us a coupla steaks, huh?'

Then he hit the switch.

* * *

The drone roared over our heads. It was smaller than I imagined, especially considerin the noise it was makin. It definitely wouldn't have been any good at sneakin up on the enemy. Then again, seein as how it was equipped with two 100lb air-to-surface wog-killer missiles as well as a laser-guided insurgent strike glide bomb, I guess it didn't need to. It was, as they say in the trade, a motherfuckin death machine. I watched as it flew straight past us and on towards the village, no more than a coupla hundred feet above the ground. Cal the retard was actually wavin at it, not realising there was nobody aboard. 'Hey!' he yelled. 'Over here!' The drone carried on, turnin slightly as it reached the village and then shot off into the desert, dissapearin behind a small mountain range in the distance. I shook my head, almost laughin. 'Well I'll be… '

As I straightened up and dusted myself down, I looked over at Cal. He was cryin again, obviously realisin his stay of execution was over. Like I said before, there ain't no cavalry out here, no charge of the light brigade. He was, in a word, fucked.

Jus' then there was a sound like thunder, and I looked to see the drone returnin towards us, flyin even faster and lower this time, with purpose. I swear to god if it'd had a face it would've been smilin. I watched in horror as it got closer and closer to the village, a plummetin feeling in the pit of my stomach as I realised what was about to happen. And then I was the retard, wavin my hands in the air, jumpin up and down and screamin 'Stop! No!'

And forgettin there was nobody there.

The drone was gone before the smoke cleared. I heard it go, even though I couldn't see anythin. It sounded lighter somehow, less menacing now that it'd dropped its load. I closed my eyes, opened them and closed them again, until eventually the air was clear enough for me to witness what I already knew.

It's funny how your mind works in times of great stress, son. As I looked at the blackened ruins that two minutes earlier had been homes, all I could think was how tidy a job it was. Seriously, it was a perfect hit; the buildings precisely flattened with almost none of the surrounding area touched. Even the farm was still standing, the goats shuffling nervously around their poles. As I watched the thick coils of black smoke spiralin up from what was left of the village, I didn't think about Gita, lyin broken in her bed, or about the children, cowerin under the tables they had set for a feast. I didn't think about little Basim, peekin up at me through a patch of berries, his cheeky face so much like yours it was frightenin. I didn't even think about Afa, about the softness of her hair or the warmth of her skin, like an unfulfilled promise crouched in the depths of those endless nights. I didn't think about them because there was no point anymore. They were all just a pile of charred bones now. Bones and ash. They were gone.

I walked over to Cal and shot him in the neck. The force took him out of his chair and into the dirt. He squirmed a little on his back, his stumps thrashin in the air as he clutched his throat, trying desperately to stem the flow. I stood over him and watched him drown in his own blood for a while before I shot him in the head. Then I started walkin.

* * *

Now that I could see him properly, Danny looked terrifying. He was still wearing his army fatigues, the dusty brown shirt ripped around the neck and spattered with dark red spots. It was his eyes I noticed most though – heavy purple rings framing bloodshot eyeballs. He looked like he hadn't slept for weeks. He looked like he wasn't there at all.

'I said ya betta get yourself cleaned up!' he shouted, his voice slurring slightly, creaking with the booze.

I licked my lips and tasted blood.

'I said GET UP!'

Somewhere inside me – in the deepest, safest place I have – I felt something shudder.

Felt you shudder.

As if you knew what was coming next.

'GET UP!'

I opened my mouth to speak, but the words wouldn't come.

'I SAID GET UP!'

I swallowed hard. 'Is that what they taught you at soldier school Dan? To hit things smaller than you? Is that how you get what you want?'

Danny took a step closer to me.

'Please Danny, listen... '

But Danny didn't want to listen.

He reached for the switch again and the lights went off.

'I'm sorry,' I said. 'I'm so sorry.'

But this time I was speaking to you.

FOUR

I walked for hours, away from Cal, the village, everythin. I walked and walked. All I had with me was the clothes on my back, my notebook in my pocket and my gun. No water. No food. It didn't make a difference. I kept walkin, the sun settin before me, smearin the sky pink and red like the bleedin gums of hell. I headed straight for them.

The sky got dark and the stars came out, the wind so cold I stopped bein able to feel my fingers or toes. I kept walkin. The moon was out that night, a big cheesy grin smirkin down on the barren nothingness all around me. For some reason it bugged the hell outta me, that moon. In fact I kinda felt like whippin out my pistol and puttin one in its eye. But I kept my hands in my pockets and my eyes on the dirt. Ain't no point pullin a gun on no celestial body, son. I reckon that there's the first, second and third signs of madness all rolled into one, ha.

As usual there weren't much to look at in that big ol' desert. I might've been on the other side of the border, but it was the same old shit keepin me company. Rocks, sand, flies. At one point a rattlesnake darted out from behind a boulder and blocked my path, shakin his tail for all he was worth. I stepped right over him and carried on, not even breakin pace. The snake dropped his tail and slithered on. I guess he sensed I was in no mood to be fucked with.

I saw the smoke just after dawn. Now I don't know if you've ever noticed before, but dawn actually begins much earlier than you'd think, long before the sun shows up to take all the credit. I mean it. If you watch the sky long and hard enough, you can sense that sunrise probably an hour and a half before that first crack of light appears over the horizon. First thing to look for is the stars startin to disappear. Not all of 'em mind. The brighter ones, the planets and shit, might stick around a while longer, but for the most part the sky starts to empty until eventually it's as black as a busted TV screen, with only the light of that no-good moon for company. After that, ya get your blues and purples movin in, the blackness of the night slowly drainin away until before you know it the sun's comin up behind ya, the sky streaked with pinks and reds and oranges and all that romantic shit that poets and artists like to mess their shorts over, but in reality are just a bunch of colours that don't mean squat.

Anyway like I said, it was just after dawn when I spotted the smoke on the horizon, a small cloud in the distance, curlin up towards the sky. I stopped walkin and watched, realisin after a few seconds that it wasn't smoke, but dust. What's more, it was getting closer.

Now normally in these situations – being approached by an unknown vehicle in hostile territory – I would make an effort to conceal myself, to get on my belly or hide behind a rock or whatever. This time however I jus' stood and waited, watchin that cloud of dust get bigger and bigger, until eventually the khaki brown of a Land Rover came into view. And I saw that it was one of ours.

* * *

My sister picked me up from the hospital. She didn't say anything when she saw me.

She didn't need to.

I let her stay for a few weeks until I was walking around again. She helped tidy up the apartment – she even offered to help me redecorate – but I was eager for her to go. Every night when I went to bed I slept with Dustin's memory stick under my pillow.

I had things I needed to take care of.

* * *

'Corporal Parker. You're a difficult man to get hold of.'

I stood open mouthed as Commander Big Bollocks killed the ignition and stepped down from the vehicle. Even with the shock of seein him out here, impeccably dressed in full service uniform despite the heat, I still felt my arm fumblin for a salute, years of drills and trainin kickin in no matter how much I tried to fight it.

'At ease Corporal,' the Commander nodded as he approached me, takin off his hat and restin it in the crook of his arm. 'I don't suppose you got a drink there? I'm drier than a nun's crack.' I shook my head, struggling to make sense of his presence here. I don't mind tellin you son, it felt like my fuckin mind was unwindin for sure. 'Not to worry,' he continued, carefully removing one of his starched white gloves and wipin his mouth with the back of his hand. 'I got an ice-cold beer waiting for me back at the base. Right now though there're a few matters we need to discuss. Isn't that right Danny?'

Suddenly my mouth was dry too, like I'd swallowed half the frickin desert or somethin – which when you thought about it I probably had. 'How'd you find me?' I finally managed to croak. The Commander smiled. 'Ah. Well, let's just say Corporal Doggerel gave us a pretty good idea where to start looking… Once he'd recuperated that is.' 'Doggie's alive?' I asked in disbelief. 'Oh, he's fine,' he chuckled. 'We picked him up about a month back. He was dehydrated and sunburnt, but alive. For now. Which is more than I can say for your unit, eh Corporal?' I swallowed hard, my throat feelin like it was about to split open. 'It was terrible,' I mumbled. 'I'm sure it was, Corporal. I find friendly fire always leaves a sour taste in one's mouth, no matter how you choose to… frame it.'

I didn't say anythin.

'I mean, you've obviously been planning this for some time. The ammunition we retrieved from the Lieutenant's body matched that stolen from the firing range at the base, so it wasn't a random attack. You didn't just lose your shit one night like most of the other freaks out here. No, you had time to think it through. Plan it. You had all your bases covered – right down to sabotaging the GPS and radio, which by the way we found buried, under your tent of all places. Very clever. But the question remains – why there? Why leave yourself marooned? What was it, a suicide mission? Because I've got to be honest with you, I never had you pegged as a coward. Crazy, sure. Homicidal, undoubtedly. Which by the way brings us around to your Staff Sergeant, Jim – found strangled with a length of cord that I'm sure closer analysis will show matches your boot laces.'

Instinctively I found myself slippin into recon mode, scannin the area for opportunities to escape, calculatin the number of footsteps it would take to reach the Land Rover.

Evidently sensing my unease, Big Bollocks reached out a hand and gave me a big, paternal slap on the arm. 'Hey, relax there Dan! I'm not here to court martial you. Shit, if I'd wanted to do that I'd have brought you in weeks ago. See we've been following you pretty closely, Corporal. Had a fix on you ever since that fat sack of shit Doggerel stumbled into my office and started whining about some damn cat he claimed you'd killed. Like I'm a goddamned animal protection officer now, huh?'

The Commander chuckled again, reachin into his blazer pocket and pullin out a preposterously large cigar, which he proceeded to light. 'Now as it happens, most of our people thought we should probably just take you out – put a bullet behind your ear and frame you as a wack-job. A couple of them even thought it'd be a good idea to put you on trial. Get the papers involved. Show the world the army has modernised. That we won't stand for this sort of thing anymore... '

He paused to contemplate the end of his cigar, belchin out a perfect, grey smoke ring that hovered before me for a second before fragmentin and fallin apart. 'Of course, these people are not politicians,' he continued. 'They don't appreciate the headaches negative press can cause us. The question's already being asked higher up. Then of course there's the anti-war lobby. Always keen to jump on a good massacre, always looking for a new angle to exploit. A fact I believe you're *intimately* aware of Corporal?'

I shuffled awkwardly, the smoke driftin from the Commander's open mouth beggin to turn my stomach.

'There's a very real worry at the top that the tide is about to turn. We're not talking about a few cranks waving flags at rallies – we're talking about full-scale insurrection. Riots, social unrest. Governments could fall. The people might be sheep, but there's only so many self-combusting soldiers they can take before the press starts moaning about taxes being used to fund a bunch of kamikaze meatheads… all offence intended, Corporal.' He paused again to laugh at his own joke then stopped, suddenly serious. 'So what do we do with you? What to do with a guy like Danny? Do we string you up by your testicles and feed you to the courts? I mean, even with the best defence in the world you're looking at gross misconduct and negligent and indiscriminate discharge of unauthorised weaponry, not to mention multiple homicides, including that of a well-loved and respected senior ranking officer. You're looking at life without parole. Maybe even the chair. I'm sure there's a whole bunch of wives and mothers who'd petition to watch you fry – women who packed their boys off to war only to get a knock on the door from a casualty notification officer a few weeks later. It's heartbreaking really.'

At this, Big Bollocks dropped his cigar and extinguished it under the heel of his boot, twisting firmly on the spot, the way you might crush a particularly unpleasant cockroach. He took a deep breath. 'But where does retribution get us at the end of the day? After all, an eye for an eye only puts the opticians out of business. And God knows if there's one thing this world needs right now, it's jobs. *Trust* me. So with all that in mind Corporal, I've made a decision.'

I waited for the click of handcuffs around my wrists.

Or the gunshot.

'You're to be decorated as a war hero.'

At this point I began to crack up. I mean it, I laughed my fuckin head off. I waited for the Commander to follow suit. But when I looked up I saw he was deadly serious.

'The people need someone they can champion during these dark days, Corporal. Someone they can look up to. Get a bit of national pride pumping for once. Next week marks the fourteenth anniversary of this godforsaken adventure. Fourteen years! Do you know how hard that is to justify to Johnny Public when you're closing his kid's school and knocking down his local hospital? Do you have any *idea* what kind of pressure it puts our poor, hardworking politicians under when they announce yet another billion dollar investment in the latest drone technology, even as we pull out our troops? Don't you think there's quite enough bad news around already with the economy and the environment without piling yet more shit on the doorstep with tales of your psychopathic exploits? No, it's been decided. You were on patrol in the desert, a peacekeeping mission, naturally, when an M-2 cell ambushed your unit. Real nasty bastards they were, fundamentalist to the core. Torched and slayed every one of you as you lay sleeping in your beds. All except you. By some *miracle*, you were spared – the sole survivor of the attack.'

'What about Doggie?' I asked.

'Ah. Well, it turns out Private Doggerel didn't make such a good recovery after all. You see there is rather a lot of animosity between you two, so perhaps it would be better for everyone involved if... Anyway, back to the story

– what does lowly old Corporal Parker do next, eh? Does he crumple into a heap of self-pity after witnessing his friends mercilessly slaughtered by a pack of bloodthirsty Monsters? Does he thump the floor at the unfairness of the world and lie in the dirt to die? Why of course not! Not the dashing and courageous Corporal Parker! No, instead he decides to go it alone, pursuing these vile beasts across the desert for weeks on end, undergoing many personal hardships and sacrifices along the way until finally – finally! – he tracks them to an abandoned village, let's say, ooh, thirty miles east of here, and engages them in a thrilling fire fight before calling in the drones to finish the job, conveniently destroying any evidence of their existence along the way…'

An involuntary image of Afa popped into my head. Her hair. Her smile. I felt my stomach tighten.

'Now what do you say? Have we got a story worth telling the world?'

I gritted my teeth. 'It's a story all right… '

'Atta boy! Now there *is* one teeny-weeny little hiccup that could cause a problem if left… untended. Your wife, Mrs Parker.'

I shook my head, thrown by the mention of your ma's name.

'Lorna? What's she got to do with anythin?'

* * *

None of the major news agencies wanted to know. At least not at first.

The first few times I rang anonymously, disguising my voice, refusing to give my name. After a week or so of getting nowhere though, I started to open up a little. I figured they probably got a hundred sob stories like me every day, so I started dangling a few juicy carrots. I told them about the attack on the airbase, that I was a soldier's wife turned bad.

I still got nowhere.

Then I mentioned Project Clearwater.
Suddenly people wanted to talk.

* * *

Big Bollocks shot me a playful grin. 'You know Danny, the press are a funny old bunch. When they make the effort to drag someone up from the gutter and crown them 'People's Champion' they like to make sure there are no skeletons hanging about that might come tumbling into the daylight once they've stuck them on the front page. Just to save them looking like assholes after the fact,' he paused, a skewed grin fixed on his face. 'The thing is, you seem to have a whole fucking graveyard in your closet.'

* * *

The next day I noticed the car parked outside my apartment.

* * *

'I don't know what you're talkin about.'

'Oh come off it! An army veteran with a war protestor for a wife? You couldn't make that shit up. Not to mention the police and hospital records, the most recent of which shows that you beat that poor bitch so badly she miscarried your first and only child together? You are one piece of work, Corporal, I'll give you that.'

* * *

One evening a reporter came to call. She brought a Starbucks coffee and little black tape recorder. She said she was interested in helping me tell my story. She said she was interested in hearing anything I had to tell her about Project Clearwater.

* * *

I felt myself leavin my body, floatin high above the desert. I looked down at the Commander, amazed by how small he looked from up there. And there was something else too, glimmerin in the distance amid the endless grey sand. A smudge of sunshine…

* * *

We spoke for a long time, the reporter and me. I told her everything I could think of. I told her about Danny. About Dustin and Jeremy. It took a long time to tell her my story.

The reporter smiled throughout, nodding politely as she sipped her coffee. When I reached the end though she looked a little disappointed. She wanted to know if I had any proof, any hard evidence I could give her. Something to make it real.

I handed her the memory stick.

As she was leaving, the reporter happened to glance in at the spare bedroom – the walls still yellow, the towels still neatly folded. 'Oh, are you expecting?' she asked.

* * *

'Of course the papers would have a field day with that kind of thing. *Hero Soldier Secret Psycho Baby Killer!* They'd eat you for breakfast… '

* * *

'I was,' I said.

* * *

I peered down, strugglin to make sense of what I was seeing. It looked like a field of yellow flowers.

* * *

It's been three months since the reporter called. I still haven't heard anything. I tried calling the agency a few times but they said that she doesn't work there anymore. I tried calling a few more times. Now they won't even answer the phone.

Every day I watch the TV.

Every day it seems there's a new war to fight.

New Monsters to kill.

I sometimes wonder if it will just go on like this forever? The fighting, the killing.

The lies.

But every day I still switch on the TV. I still open the papers.

And I hope.

* * *

'The bottom line is we couldn't risk that kind of bad publicity. Not after so much planning and preparation. Anyway, we decided to fix the problem. As of… ' he paused to look at his watch.

* * *

There is a knock at the door.

* * *

'… Now. There we go, all sorted. Naturally the police and medical records have been taken care of too. All things considered I'd say you've come out of this smelling pretty good, wouldn't you agree Corporal? Corporal?'

But I wasn't listenin to him son. Not really. Because at that exact moment I'd just realised exactly what it was I'd been lookin at. And it wasn't yellow flowers I'd seen. Nah. It was a field of maize.

In one fluid motion I reached into my jacket and pulled out my gun, firin my last remainin bullet into the Commander's skull. Right between the eyes. He stood there for a moment, blinkin like he couldn't quite believe what had just happened. Then he fell down on the floor, dead. Very calmly I placed the empty gun down next to his body. Then I started walkin.

It took me longer than I thought to reach the field. By the time I got here the sun was already high in the sky and my shirt was stuck to my back. I stopped at the edge, starin in amazement at the huge stalks towerin high above my head. Just like in my dream. I sat down and took out my notebook. That was a few hours ago. I'm still here now, tryin to work out how to finish this. I guess there're a whole lot of things I should probably say. Then again, I guess by now it's too late for sayin most of them. I wish I was better with words. In a minute I will dig a small ditch with my hands and place this book inside. I've got your picture here too – the one you would have drawn if you'd had the chance. You know seein it again, I have to admit it looks kinda nice. Sand castles an' all. I wouldn't have minded vistin there one time. With you and your mother. Like a real family.

I fold the picture in two and put it in with this diary. In a second I'll cover them both with dirt. Like a smothered seed, waitin to explode. Or a bomb.

Ha.

Once the hole is filled I'll stand up, dust off my hands and walk into the corn. And just like in my dream I'll start runnin, faster and faster, switchin directions until I have no idea where I came in, or how to get out. And it won't matter. And eventually I will stop, right in the centre of the field. And I will fall to my knees as if I am about to cry.

Or pray.

AUTHOR QUESTIONNAIRE

When and why did you start writing? What inspired you to write Real Monsters*?*
I remember winning a writing competition when I was five or six with a story called *Why I Feel So Sad*. I guess that set the tone for everything that was to follow. As a teenager I was an unashamed lit-groupie. My bedroom wall was plastered with posters of Charles Bukowski, Jack Kerouac, Hubert Selby Jr., Hunter S. Thompson. Those guys were my rock stars. I'd walk around with a notebook stuffed in my pocket and order straight rye whiskey while my friends sat around drinking bottles of Smirnoff Ice. It was a deeply embarrassing period for everyone involved.

I didn't actually start writing fiction with any serious conviction until I was twenty-three or twenty-four. I was at university by then and had a two-year-old son. I was, and am, a pretty shy, anxious person, and I found writing acted as a buffer between me and the world. Something I could hide behind. There was an alternative lit blog called Straight from the Fridge that put out my first stories, and another called Beat the Dust. Those gave me the confidence that someone somewhere might be interested in my words, so I carried on, trying to improve my writing and figure out who I am. I'm still not sure I've ever topped *Why I Feel So Sad* though.

As for *Real Monsters*, the seed for the idea came from a Nietzsche quote I read on a t-shirt or a beer mat or something (which as far as I can tell is the only place anyone reads

Nietzsche these days.) It was along the lines of: 'Beware that, when fighting monsters, you yourself do not become a monster.' The idea seemed to resonate with the geo-political car crash that we, the West, have been involved in ever since September 11. I was keen to explore the de-humanising effect that war and violence have on the individual and so, rather than writing about any specific conflict I thought it might be interesting to write about literal monsters. From there I just sort of ran with it...

How do you feel modern warfare is portrayed in fiction? And did this directly impact your writing?

I have to be honest and say that, with very few exceptions, I don't like books about modern warfare. With no disrespect towards Andy McNab or Tom Clancy or any of those guys (and it is almost exclusively guys), I feel there's an unfortunate tendency to fetishise certain aspects of militaria; the weapons, the vehicles, the protocol and stuff. I'm not interested in that at all. As a kid I never played with guns. I hate those creepy shoot-a-terrorist-save-the-nation video games that seem to have rendered the plumbers and hedgehogs of the world redundant. In fact I deplore violence full stop – which probably makes writing *Real Monsters* an odd choice!

The other problem with most fictional books on this subject is that they make war seem glamorous and exciting, without capturing how mundane and detached the reality of modern warfare is. Throughout my novel, Danny repeatedly moans about the fact he's had all this training but hasn't even seen the enemy – let alone had a chance to fight them. There's no opportunity for him to live out these mythological acts of heroism he's been raised on because so much of war is technology driven these days. I guess it goes back to video games again; guys in offices on the other side of the world with a joystick and a shoot button. At least it does for those nations lucky enough to have a multi-trillion-pound defence budget at their disposal.

Real Monsters *portrays the impact of war on people both home and abroad. How important was it to you to portray this accurately?*

In some ways it's easy to forget that Britain has been involved in a near continuous cycle of foreign conflict for the last three decades. The Falklands, the Gulf War, Bosnia, Kosovo, Afghanistan, Iraq, Libya and now the current military intervention against ISIS. That's my whole life. My kids are nine and four and they've literally never known peace. Yet the literary response – particularly in Britain – has been slow to explore this trend towards violence. Whereas World War II and Vietnam provoked iconic literary, cinematic and musical responses, reactions to recent military conflicts have been more muted. Perhaps this is due to the fact these wars have taken place on foreign soil, with only the media and occasional acts of terrorism to remind us they are taking place at all? Perhaps it's too easy to close our eyes and pretend they're not happening?

As an eighteen-year-old during the 2003 Stop the War protests in London, I experienced first-hand the public enthusiasm for a peaceful resolution to the imminent Iraq war. I also experienced the subsequent disappointment, confusion and political disengagement in the decade that followed the march – a feeling compounded by revelations that further blurred the ethical lines dividing us and the bad guys. The failure to find WMDs, the torture at Abu Ghraib, the leaks by whistleblowers such as Chelsea Manning and Edward Snowden. For me, the failure of the Stop the War protests was the turning point in recent British history. It was the moment that all of the optimism and energy of those early Blair years finally dissipated and an entire generation realised that the version of democracy we're presented with is little more than a hollow promise, a sleight of hand. I mean, if a million people mobilising and saying 'No!' didn't make any difference, how can we trust this system to value our opinion on anything?

Of course the real tragedy is that rather than getting angry we lost hope. We collectively rolled over and buried our heads in booze and reality TV and just let them get on with it – which was easy to do because bombs weren't being dropped on our nurseries and hospitals. And just so long as it wasn't your child, or sibling, or parent, being sent over to be blown apart by an IED, then it was as easy to forget it was happening as switching over the channel, or flipping a page in the newspaper. But these conflicts don't happen in a vacuum. You can't intensively train people to kill, send them into incredibly stressful situations and then expect them to come home and carry on where they left off – the surge in veterans suffering from mental health issues is testament to that. Ultimately, I guess I'm keen to draw attention to the corrosive effect that war has on us as a global community, and to show that all of us are ultimately poorer when we advocate violence over diplomacy.

Your narrative gives equal weight to both the female and male narrators. Did you feel it was important to show the impact of warfare on both genders? Was this challenging?
War is usually portrayed as a predominantly masculine pursuit. In fact, if you look at some of our culture's most famous narratives about military conflict they tend to either sideline women in the story, or exclude them altogether. With *Real Monsters* I felt it was important to show the impact of conflict on both genders, exploring the transformative effects of war not just on the soldiers, but also on their relationships; how in many ways the burden is just as great for the soldier's partner, not just while they're away fighting overseas, but once they've returned home too. For some people the conflict never really ends.

While there were aspects of writing from a woman's perspective I found challenging, in some senses it was actually easier than writing Danny's parts. It was certainly less emotionally draining. For one thing, I'm actually far more aligned with Lorna's worldview and therefore I found I could get into her head more easily than Danny's – though I'm sure my wife grew sick of me constantly asking, 'But would a woman say/think that?' I was also determined to present her as a strong, independent character rather than yet another token female victim – despite the fact she is ultimately a victim of male brutality.

Danny's voice on the other hand came to me in a white-hot fever. I wrote his parts first, and very quickly. At times it felt more like performing an exorcism than writing. I used a variety of techniques to try and capture his brutal, disaffected voice. Some parts I dictated to tape or hammered out on an old keyboard, which ensured I wasn't hijacked by auto-correct. The lack of a backspace key also helped me not look backwards and just plough on until I'd got it all out. I found a lot of Danny's story incredibly uncomfortable to write – the misogyny, the homophobia, the casual racism – and I knew I had to get it down before self-doubt got the better of me. While the language Danny uses is authentic of the stories of soldiers I know who've returned from duty, as well as a certain strand of Angry White Men I've been around most of my life, it didn't make it any easier to see scratched out in ink and paper. Still, I guess that's what happens when you set out to write a book about monsters.

Why did you choose to leave the locations in the novel ambiguous?

Despite the political and cultural complexities of the type of international conflicts described in *Real Monsters*, large portions of the media are nevertheless content to impose propagandistically simple narratives when reporting them, reducing them to 'goodies and baddies', 'heroes and villains', 'us and them'. Often they read more like fairy stories, with an eternal struggle between good and evil at their heart – though which side is which depends on who's telling the story. What's more, it's always the same narrative. An interesting exercise is to take a news story covering an overseas conflict and remove all of the proper nouns. Try it. It doesn't matter who's being blown up or shot at or where it's happening – the story is always the same. The language and the tone are identical. It's tragic, actually, the cyclical nature of war. The same old atrocities occur again and again across generations – it's just the names that change.

With *Real Monsters*, I made a conscious decision to reflect the broad brushstrokes adopted by the popular press. I imagined it as a sort of shadow play, with the narrative stripped right down to its base elements. Man lost in desert hunts faceless enemy. He could be a knight hunting dragons or an American G.I. fighting the Taliban. The important thing for me was capturing the universal human element at the heart of a conflict, with the focus on individuals rather than nations. I felt placing the action anywhere too specific would hinder that aim. You'll notice it's not just Danny's story that has a stock 'desert' background. Lorna too lives in a non-specific 'Western city.' It could be London, but it could equally be New York or Sydney or even Paris or Berlin. That amorphous approach to place extends to Danny's accent. He could be a Texan or a Cockney, or even Brummie – I guess it just depends who's reading it.

Describe your average writing day.

Like most writers, I don't have the luxury of writing fiction full time. Living in a house is an expensive pursuit, and as a result I spend most daylight hours in an office, writing copy. The majority of my writing is done in the cracks between my work and family life. Before breakfast and on my lunch break. In condensation in the shower and in the dirt on my windscreen. I guess sleep is the biggest sacrifice, as I'm often up until the early hours, rattling away.

Mostly this is fine, as I tend to feel a bit lost when I'm not busy. With *Real Monsters*, though, I think I came pretty close to losing my mind on a number of occasions. Danny's head was a pretty horrendous place to spend any amount of time. Several times my wife woke up to find me crouched in the bottom of a wardrobe, muttering obscenities into a tape recorder. Or else I'd wake the kids up by screaming or shouting at the screen. It was a difficult time for everyone. I've made a promise to them that I'll try and get less emotionally involved in the next thing I write. Having said that, I've already made plans to spend a few nights sleeping rough in the local park, so I'll guess we'll just have to see what happens.

What are you working on next?

I'm writing another novel at the moment, called *Wild Life.* It tells the story of a troubled advertising salesman who abandons his family and takes to sleeping rough in a local park, where he's befriended by a secret fraternity of homeless men who are living out a utopian rural fantasy. They grow their own food, hunt squirrels and foxes, that sort of thing – until of course the real world intervenes and it all falls to pieces. I suppose it's sort of like *The Beach* transposed to an inner-city park, or *Lord of the Flies* played out by middle-aged men.

Although stylistically it's far more conventional than *Real Monsters*, it still touches on a number of the same themes: bullying, greed, violence. I guess at it's core is the idea that humanity is just a veneer, that beneath the suit and tie, we're all really just animals, capable of acts of immeasurable cruelty. While I realise that all makes it sound pretty heavy, it's actually a lot of fun. It's certainly less exhausting to write than *Real Monsters*, though I have to admit I'm nervous about being in the park at night. Or rather, I'm nervous about the things that might be in the park with me...

ACKNOWLEDGMENTS

Neither I nor this novel would be here without the encouragement and support of the following people: Dad, Mum, Aidan Gorbanzo, Ciara Smyth, Lauren Smith, the Browns, Laidlaws, O'Raffertys, Smyths, McGowan-Smyths, Barbers, Oakleys, Carrolls, Flynns and my family in Cebu, Freelance Mourners, Injured Party, Red Shirt, Adelle Stripe, Ben Myers, James Hawes, Michael Langan, Nina Rapi, Sam Mills, the Lynchs, Mov Jones, Colin Hammer, Team SAM, Riz Khan @ RK Animation, Gem Sidnell @ Moo Moo Art & Photgraphy, Writing West Midlands & all at Room 204, the de Rohan family, the Bitmead family and all at Legend Press.

Finally, special thanks go to Elliot, Felix and Simone for their unconditional love and endless patience. I'm sorry about the cat.

COME AND VISIT US AT
WWW.LEGENDPRESS.CO.UK

FOLLOW US
@LEGEND_PRESS